MW01143034

OF CUSTOMS AND EXCISE

OF CUSTOMS AND EXCISE
Short Fiction

by

RACHNA MARA

For
Lakshmi and Shakuntala
and
Karen and Robin

The author wishes to thank the Explorations Program of The Canada Council
and the Ontario Arts Council for their assistance.

CANADIAN CATALOGUING IN PUBLICATION DATA
Mara, Rachna
Of Customs and Excise
ISBN 0-929005-25-2

I. Title.

PS8576.A7304 1991   C813'.54   C91-094896-8
PR9199.3.M304 1991

Copyright © 1991 by Rachna Mara

Printed and bound in Canada

Edited by Charis Wahl
Cover illustration by Rossitza Skortcheva Penney
Second Story Press gratefully acknowledges the assistance of
the Ontario Arts Council and The Canada Council

Published by
SECOND STORY PRESS
760 Bathurst Street
Toronto, Ontario
M5S 2R6

CONTENTS

Pipal Leaves

WHISPERS OF COOL on her body, green fields, rolling meadows, soft, misty trees – she was back in Staffordshire. As her eyes half-opened, they focused dimly on the naked light bulb dangling from the ceiling. She closed her eyes, drifted across Mr. Alton-Croft's field, moist, lush, the hedgerows at the periphery glistening with blackberries. She climbed the stile separating the field from the road, and there she was, in Barundabad. Dust swirls, scratching hands, dark faces. Amongst them was Dr. Kamla Naigar, listening to the heartbeat of a cow. Huddled under the cow, a purple-clad figure, face covered in the *pulloo* of her sari. Dr. Naigar turned towards Bridget, held out a dish of *gulab jamun*. "Here, Bigshot White Sahib. Eat this." Bridget shook her head, but Dr. Naigar forced her face upwards, dropped towards her mouth a blob of feces.

She sat up, wet with perspiration, heart pounding. Wisps of the nightmare lingered; Dr. Naigar's dark face, the veiled hostility replaced with open anger.

Everyday she was more reluctant to go to the clinic.

She straightened quickly; there was no time for self-pity or self-doubt. Back in England, she'd had few doubts about the Voluntary Service Overseas. India had been the logical choice; she'd been born here, British India then, lived here her first six years.

Her memories of those years had been hazy, based more on general impressions, stories repeated by her parents than on actual recall. It wasn't until her arrival here that she'd fully understood how little those shadows reflected reality. Pressing, invasive heat, wrenching stomach complaints, the language, and, most of all, the local customs, baffling, unyielding.

And there was Dr. Naigar.

Impatiently, she dragged her hair off her face, shone her flashlight on the floor. Nothing. She shook out her shoes, one of the first things she'd been taught. This was a country of lurking dangers, flashing, darting tongues and tails.

In the toilet, breathing through her mouth to minimize the stench, she flicked on the light. A movement in the corner caught her eye. It was a harmless lizard skittering up the wall, its skin greenish-beige, its scales capturing miniature rainbows. She positioned her feet on the raised footpads on either side of the hole, and squatted awkwardly. The first morning walk she'd taken down the muddy path to the clinic had markedly reduced her distaste for her own toilet facilities. She'd seen a boy sitting on his haunches. She'd smiled and waved, then realized what it was that coiled to the ground, brown, snake-like.

In the bathroom, Asha, her servant girl, had left a bucket of water in the corner. Bridget, now accustomed to bathing Indian style, dipped a *lota* in the bucket, sloshed herself with water, quickly soaped and rinsed.

Kamla Naigar would probably be at the clinic by now. No matter how early Bridget was, Dr. Naigar was earlier. In the clinic, she was pervasive. Dr. Naigar, her sari sloppy with a crooked hem and an uneven *pulloo*, cleaning the tables with slovenly, languid movements, yet missing nothing; Dr. Naigar, her dry voice filtering through the curtain between their examining rooms, translating, *Dr. Parkinson, the patient is talking about a pain in her stomach not her chest;* Dr. Naigar, diagnosing the villagers' ailments with casual speed, dispensing herbal concoctions that, surprisingly, worked; Dr. Naigar, her dark, slightly pocked face expressionless, barely glancing at Bridget, thwarting every attempt at modernization, smothering every suggestion.

❖

That first day at the clinic, as she'd surveyed the bare walls, the

8

cement floor, she'd known it would be a challenge working here, but she'd never doubted that she could contribute.

"Since this is your first time, we will work together," Dr. Naigar said. "Next week you can start on your own."

The first patient was a six-year-old boy, his scrawny back covered with boils, oozing pus.

"Why did you not bring him sooner?" Bridget asked, in halting Hindi.

The boy's mother giggled, hid her mouth with her hands, stared shyly yet frankly at Bridget, examining her strangeness. "It's only a few boils, Doctorsahib."

"But see, if you had brought him in sooner, it would be easier to make better."

"But they weren't so bad before."

"He's going to need an antibiotic, wouldn't you say, Dr. Naigar?"

Dr. Naigar cleaned the infected area with small, ineffectual dabs, smeared a greenish paste on the boils, and covered each of them with a leaf.

"What's that?" said Bridget coldly in English.

"Pipal leaves." Dr. Naigar turned to the boy's mother. "Now come back two days from now for a repeat. Understand, two days."

The mother nodded, grinned shyly at Bridget, "Thank you, Doctorsahib."

After they'd gone, Bridget said, "Surely, Doctor, an antibiotic would have been appropriate."

Dr. Naigar unhurriedly wiped the bench with an antiseptic solution. Her voice was lazy. "Doctorsahib, you are not the only one knowing how to practice medicine. We peasants are knowing a few things also."

Bridget's face reddened.

"Even if we decide he needs our supply of antibiotics, who is going to see he takes them?"

"His mother, of course."

"His mother cannot read. She has five other children, and she is working in the fields, washing clothes, fetching water, grinding flour and cooking. She will not remember instructions about medicine.

9

Then she will be afraid to tell us, so she will give him the rest of the tablets all at once or she will be throwing them out."

"But we must educate her to the necessity of giving the tablets. We have to. After all, it is the most effective treatment."

Dr. Naigar motioned Kunti, the nurse, to send in the next patient.

Outside, the drizzle changed to a torrential downpour. Bridget's stomach, still churning after an unusually hot breakfast, had gone into painful spasm.

The boy's back had healed in a week.

Since that first day, Dr. Naigar had never again launched into explanations. She'd continued to practice her peculiar brand of medicine and grimly ignored Bridget, except for occasionally calling out treatments through the curtain separating their examining rooms.

Yesterday afternoon, Dr. Naigar's careful indifference had slipped.

There'd been two patients left, both of whom had insisted on seeing the white, foreign doctor. Anxious not to permit the slight, Bridget had requested Dr. Naigar's assistance.

Dr. Naigar had openly disputed her treatment for the patient's dysentery, insisting instead on one of her herbal remedies. Bridget had given way because she wouldn't argue in front of a patient, but afterwards she'd confronted Dr. Naigar.

Dr. Naigar had lashed like a scorpion. "Listen, Bigshot White Sahib, you don't find things modern enough, you go home. We don't want interfering. You British have caused enough trouble already."

Bridget dressed hurriedly and tied her mousy hair high above her neck.

She should have stood her ground, despite the presence of the patient. *Bigshot White Sahib.*

Bloody wog.

She bit her lip, hurried into the kitchen. Lighting a fire in the earthen fireplace, she boiled water for tea and heated the remnants of last night's meal.

In the small front room, she wrapped a piece of *chapati* around the potato *bhaji* and bit cautiously. Immediately, her eyes watered. She swallowed, gulped a mouthful of tea, scalding her mouth.

She would not let Dr. Naigar's pettiness divert her from the work at hand, or distort her motives for being here. She hadn't come to India out of missionary zeal – Great White Doctor bringing civilization. She'd just wanted to contribute.

She was chewing too hard. She wasn't personally responsible for the tyranny of the Raj, dead and gone ten years ago, or for the villagers' fascination with her skin.

Once, in the clinic, she'd overheard a mother tell her small daughter, "See, when God made us, he formed us out of dough, and put us in the oven to bake. And some, he took out at the proper time, and they came out just right, nice and brown like us. But others he left in too long and they got a bit burnt. And then he became worried and overcareful, so he ended up taking out some people too soon, before they were properly cooked. And that is Doctorsahib's kind."

Bridget smiled. It had poured rain since she got here, and even when it was sunny, she didn't tan, just freckled, then burned and peeled.

"*Namaste*, Doctorsahib." Asha had silently crept in and stood grinning at her.

"*Namaste*."

A scrawny nineteen-year-old, Asha looked more like fourteen, but was hard-working and efficient. She kept Bridget's tiny bungalow spotless, fetched water from the well, washed her clothes, cooked her meals. Perfectly cooked except for one thing. Asha was always friendly, smiling, nodding, but despite Bridget's attempts, the food remained bitingly hot. Lately, she had the uneasy feeling that maybe Asha understood more than she let on.

Hastily, she picked up her umbrella and bag and strode towards the clinic. Was that a typical white reaction to a brown face, chronic distrust? It was so corroding, this perpetual doubt.

Already, the early morning cool was waning, and moisture from last night's rain rose in swirls.

People crouched outside their huts, some cleaning their teeth with Neem twigs, some hacking up phlegm, spitting. Women scoured pots, coaxed fires, sat with babies at their breasts. Others balanced pots of water on their heads, their glass bangles gleaming red, purple, blue, the occasional flash of gold. Children, mostly naked, ran around squealing, and there were the inevitable figures behind bushes as well as the clusters of children squatting more openly, accompanied by halos of flies.

"*Namaste*, Doctorsahib, *namaste*," they called as she passed. Smoke curled upwards, adding to the pungent odours of moist earth, food, sewage. Cows wandered, chewing tufts of grass, garbage, scattering fresh droppings, which the women would later scrape up for fuel. Voices sang, chattered, argued, and a radio blared Hindi film music.

Even now, the sights, sounds, and smells evoked contradictory sensations – distaste, frustration at the poverty, the fatalism; admiration for the resilience, the exuberance.

She veered onto the path leading to the clinic. On her right, at some distance from the village, sprawled the large bungalow belonging to the richest *zamindar* family, the Ungolis.

Bridget had met them soon after her arrival, when they'd invited her and Dr. Naigar to dinner. They'd been eager to meet her, mostly, Bridget suspected, to establish their superiority over the peasant villagers and to practice their English. At that dinner, too, Dr. Naigar had managed to disconcert her.

The meal had been long, heavy, rich. They'd been seated on the matted floor, whilst the new daughter-in-law of the house, Parvati, had served the food she'd cooked. The bride, draped in gold and purple silk, head and face modestly covered, did not eat with them, but kept their plates, particularly Bridget's, piled with food, despite her protests.

Bridget, squirming discreetly to restore her circulation, tried to conceal her annoyance at the intrusive hospitality. Mrs. Ungoli, the *zamindar*'s wife, droned on about the academic successes of their homely eldest son, Mohan, the modern conveniences of their house, and the inadequacies of their many servants. Dr. Naigar prolonged the meal by eating gargantuan quantities and uttering long, fulsome compliments. Bridget had the distinct impression that Dr. Naigar was amused by her discomfort.

For dessert, the bride carried in a bowl of *gulab jamun*. Bridget didn't care for the sickly brown dumplings, and was about to refuse firmly when she caught the bride's eye. Something about the glance puzzled her, made her pause. Long enough for Dr. Naigar, perfectly aware of Bridget's dislike, to say, "*Gulab jamun*, very nice. It is your favourite, no, Dr. Parkinson?"

The bride smiled, gave Bridget a large helping.

As they walked away from the Ungoli house, Dr. Naigar remarked, as though addressing the sky, "In an Indian house, the bride always has to prove her cooking prowess. Parvati is a good cook, no?" She burst into laughter.

❖

Bridget quickened her step. She'd have to learn to confront Dr. Naigar, whether there were people around or not.

"Good morning, Dr. Naigar." She forced her voice to sound normal.

Dr. Naigar, absorbed in filling a bottle with Mercurochrome, grunted.

As usual, Dr. Naigar's cotton sari was unevenly tied, her dark, oiled hair twisted in a bun that threatened to unwind, but somehow never did. Bridget's fingers itched to push in the two hairpins sticking halfway out of the bun. She tucked in the stray ends of her own hair.

Dr. Naigar's face seemed darker than usual. It contrasted sharply with her pale yellow sari.

Would she find it easier to confront Dr. Naigar if she were white? Would she find the situation less intolerable, feel no need to say anything? Bridget's hands fumbled as she took down a jar of disinfectant from the cupboard. She forced herself to collect her supplies slowly, reminding herself that the silence was quite normal. She carried her tray to her table, and Dr. Naigar drew the curtain between their examining rooms.

A couple of hours later, as she summoned a patient in the waiting room, a voice said in English, "Good morning, Dr. Parkinson."

It was Mrs. Ungoli, the *zamindar*'s wife. Next to her sat the bride, Parvati, clad in bright blue silk, an exotic bird amongst brown sparrows. As usual, her face and head were covered by the *pulloo* of her sari.

Mrs. Ungoli heaved herself to her feet. "I am wanting you to examine Parvati," she whispered loudly.

"Yes, of course, one of us will see you as soon as your number comes up."

"No, no, I am wanting only you to examine her. You are knowing the latest."

Bridget flushed. Even in a whisper, Mrs. Ungoli's voice carried.

"Very well, I'll get to you when your turn comes."

Mrs. Ungoli looked offended.

An hour later, Mrs. Ungoli came in with her daughter-in-law.

The girl was clearly uneasy, her head low, the hand holding the *pulloo* clenched hard.

"Now then, what seems to be the problem?" Bridget said to the girl.

"Oh, I do not think there is any problem," smiled Mrs. Ungoli. "Parvati has just missed a few. The silly girl did not want to come, but we are knowing modern ways. We want you to examine her and confirm."

Bridget suppressed her irritation at the mother-in-law's presence. Family relationships were different here.

"Well, the best thing is to have a pregnancy test done, but since the sample will have to go to Najgulla, the results will take a few days."

"Yes, yes, we can do that, but we are also wanting you to examine her now."

"Very well."

She motioned the bride to the bench behind the screen. Mrs.

14

Ungoli hovered, buzzing and twittering as the girl unwound rustling yards of silk, lay down on the bench. She was smooth, lovely, but her lips were bloodless, her body rigid. Mrs. Ungoli stood like a tombstone over her, talking incessantly.

"Mrs. Ungoli, I'd like you to wait on the other side of the screen."

Mrs. Ungoli opened her mouth to argue, but Bridget gently manoeuvred her around.

She palpated the bride's lower abdomen.

"Do try to relax. It won't hurt, I just want to see how far along you are."

There it was, the uterus budding upwards. She measured its outmost tip.

"When did you last have your menses?"

The girl swallowed. Finally a squeak, "I don't know."

"Well, not to worry." This was one part of her practice she enjoyed. It was important for an Indian bride to produce children; being pregnant would raise her status – particularly if she bore a boy.

She listened with her stethoscope for a fetal heartbeat. There it was, faint but unmistakable.

"Congratulations. You're pregnant, all right. I'd say, about four months, anyway."

The girl's body went slack, her eyes closed. Mrs. Ungoli's smile disappeared like an eclipse.

"What nonsense is this?" Dr. Naigar spoke sharply as she pushed past the curtain into Bridget's examining room.

The blood drained from Bridget's face. She said in her coldest voice, "Doctor, I believe I can manage."

Dr. Naigar's glance was furious, contemptuous.

She forced Bridget to the foot of the bench and examined Parvati.

"Dr. Parkinson, this girl is clearly no more that two or three months' pregnant. You English doctors think you are knowing everything, but you cannot even determine how far along a woman is?"

She spoke rapidly in Hindi to Mrs. Ungoli. Bridget caught the phrase, "Crazy woman, new at it...."

She'd heard a fetal heartbeat. There was no question the girl was in her second trimester. As she moved towards Dr. Naigar, she felt the bride's eyes on her. It was same curious glance she'd seen the evening she'd dined with the Ungolis.

Abruptly she said, "I'll examine her again."

"There is no need for that," snapped Dr. Naigar. "I have already corrected your mistake."

Bridget said slowly, "I am examining her again, Doctor. She is my patient."

She placed the stethoscope on the bride's lower abdomen, listened.

"I'm afraid I mistook intestinal gurglings for a heartbeat." Her voice was tight, clipped. "It's difficult to say how far along she is, but certainly no more than two or three months."

Parvati went limp, her eyes blank. Dr. Naigar grunted. Her fingers fiddled with the hairpins in her bun.

Mrs. Ungoli said shrilly, "You are sure now?"

"I'm certain. I'm not accustomed to using this kind of stethoscope, but that's no excuse. I apologize for my error."

Mrs. Ungoli's face relaxed. "Oh, yes, it is ancient equipment. And you are also working too hard, Dr. Parkinson. She is going to have to get more rest, no, Dr. Kamla?"

Bridget was only peripherally aware of Parvati tying her sari with clumsy hands, while Dr. Naigar and Mrs. Ungoli chattered in Hindi.

As they left the clinic, huddled under their umbrellas, she heard Dr. Naigar's voice, low, expressionless, "Thank you, Doctor."

The rain had stopped by the time the last patient left and Kunti, the nurse, departed.

Despite the overhead fan, the room was muggy. Bridget's stomach burned, her head swam. The clinic was silent except for the rattle of instruments Dr. Naigar gathered.

"How long has she been married?"

Dr. Naigar, her back to Bridget, continued to collect the instruments. "Three months."

Bridget leaned against the table.

"Do you know what happens if they find out she is more than three months pregnant?" Dr. Naigar's hands, suspended above the tray, gleamed with steel. "There'll be an accident, screams in the night. They'll say her sari caught fire while she was frying something, or she ate poisoned food put out for rats."

Bridget's stomach cramped. She saw a peacock-blue figure bobbing under a vulturous black umbrella, saw Parvati's eyes on her again, the eyes of a cornered bird, knowing there is no reprieve.

She cleared her throat. "Thank you, Doctor."

Dr. Naigar put the instruments down with a clatter. "There's a lot to learn, no?" She spoke softly, but her eyes were still hard.

Bridget nodded. She glimpsed a face in the spotted mirror over the sink. It took a few seconds to recognize it as her own – it was so pale.

Asha's Gift

Asha LAGGED ON THE WAY to Doctorsahib's. She stopped to exchange quips with Chuddi, who was scrubbing pots outside her hut, then hurried to the bungalow without picking the brilliant hibiscus she usually gathered for her hair. She must not let the Angrezi Doctorsahib think she was afraid to face her. But Doctorsahib had already left her bungalow for the clinic.

Asha fumbled with the key tied to the end of her sari, and unlocked the door. Everything was just the way Doctorsahib always left it – a few dishes in the front room, the water gone from the bucket in the bathroom, bed unmade, dirty clothes in the basket in the corner of the bedroom. No indications as to Doctorsahib's state of mind.

Asha gathered the dishes from the front room, stalked into the kitchen, and clunked them into the basin. She picked up the broom and started to sweep, glass bangles tinkling discordantly.

These Angrezi-log, what arrogance they had! Why hadn't Doctorsahib Parkinson said anything yesterday? She'd caught Asha red-handed and she'd said nothing except, "I do not have time now. I will talk to you tomorrow." She'd said it in Hindi, of course, her awful Hindi, with that *pah-pa-pah-pa-pah* voice that Asha and all the villagers made so much fun of.

It was a mistake, agreeing to work for this Angrezi doctor. So many strange ways she had. The way she spoke. The clothes she wore, such dull colours. And her skin. Not nice and fair so much as boiled-looking, with ugly, dark blotches. Her eyes were pale and watery, and she had no eyelashes to speak of, just a few scrubby, straight hairs, like a cow.

At the Ungoli house, at least you knew where you were. Ungoli Memsahib might be a terror, but she didn't toy with you like a cat with a mouse. If Ungoli Memsahib caught you at anything, she gave you a quick, hard slap, and that was the end of it.

I will talk to you tomorrow. Asha spat on the dishes in the basin. And again. She scooped up the dirt, half-considered dumping it in Doctorsahib's bed, then swept it vigorously outside.

❖

She'd been working for the Ungolis when Doctorsahib Kamla told her about the new Angrezi doctor coming to the village, asked if she was interested in doing her housework. Asha'd had enough of working for the Ungolis.

Burra Memsahib always sat on the cot at the head of the courtyard, watching everybody with a serpent's eye. Mean, she was, grudging every bite the servants took. True, she handed down the odd bit of worn clothing, which came in handy for Asha and for Sundri, her sister, and Sundri's two children. But for the clothes Asha would never have stayed.

Yes, she would have. She would have had to. Sundri's husband, Tilak, was always complaining, complaining about having an extra mouth to feed. He never noticed the cleaning, mending, cooking, fetching water from the well, even helping in the field. All he noticed was an extra mouth to feed. Particularly since the day behind the bushes. She'd shown him the knife, described what she'd do. He'd never bothered her again. But there were other ways.

"Why does that girl have to live with us all the time?" he'd shout at Sundri. "She's always eating, eating, eating. Why can't she get married? One woman's enough."

Sundri, hands fluttering, would say, "You knew when you married me that she was going to live with us. Where will she go, no mother and father? You promised Dr. Kamla Sahib when she gave you my dowry that my sister would also be welcome here."

"Yes, but that was years ago, and she's still here. I didn't think I'd have the girl forever. Look at her, nineteen and still not married."

"How can she get married with no dowry, you tell me that? All our extra money you drink away, so how can she get married?"

And Asha would shriek, "I will never get married, never."

"You see, you see," Tilak would yell. "There's your sister. Wanting to live off somebody else's hard work. There are boys willing enough to marry her and Dr. Kamla Sahib will provide a dowry, but—"

"Dr. Kamla Sahib has done enough for our family. I will not ask her."

The arguments always ended with Tilak hitting Sundri and Sundri crying.

In the end, Asha had found work with the Ungolis. The servants hated it there, but with the uncertainty of the rains, the cost of borrowing money for seed and tools, most of the village families were glad of any steady income, however slight. So when old Rukhma died, Asha had quickly applied for her job. Tilak had still complained, even though she handed over every rupee she earned.

Now she was grateful to Dr. Kamla Sahib for offering the opportunity to her first. There wasn't a lot in the village that Dr. Kamla Sahib didn't know about. She'd always kept an eye on Sundri and Asha; she'd looked after them in Najgulla, brought them to Barunda-bad. She'd watched out for them ever since that time, long ago.

❖

"Eat, you must eat," Dr. Kamla Sahib says to Sundri in Najgulla Hospital. Sundri is silent, creeping back to the bed their mother died in.

Asha eats everything she's given. The patients complain she even steals their food. The knife she carries makes them uneasy.

"You must stop doing that," Dr. Kamla Sahib says, bandaging the gashes on Asha's arms and legs. Asha says nothing, later, does it again. She feels only a fierce exultation as the knife cuts her skin. How to explain to Dr. Kamla Sahib, this is a preparation for returning to the streets? Any day now, they'll really be on their own. No doll, no mother or father. Towards the end, it was her mother's anguish for them that was the real burden.

❖

It hadn't taken Asha long to sum up the new doctor. She said *aap* to Asha as though she were an equal, instead of the familiar *tum*. She requested, never ordered and always said *shukria*, thank you. She never locked up food, the flour, sugar, rice, *dahls*, and she even gave Asha a key to the tiny bungalow.

The only thing Doctorsahib was fussy about was keeping the place clean. She examined corners, insisted everything be properly dusted, mopped. She hated dirt as much as the heat.

Such a small place, so easy to keep clean. Asha's body didn't ache the way it used to at the Ungolis', and she was paid a little more. And no one to watch her. At the Ungolis' with *Burra* Memsahib and all those people scurrying around, it had been impossible to search the bureau drawers and cupboards, let alone help herself to even a handful of rice.

But the best thing about working for Doctorsahib was her Hindi. It was so funny, her accent more than anything else.

It came in particularly handy over the food. Doctorsahib couldn't stand anything hot. As she ate, her eyes would stream, her face turn red. She would struggle to say, "*Khana tikha hai*, the food is hot."

And it was easy to think she'd said, "*Khana theek hai*, the food is fine."

Asha would smile, say, "*Theek hai*, Doctorsahib, *shukria*."

Then another day, Doctorsahib would try again, "*Itna lal mirchi nahi dalo*. Don't put in so many red chilies." She would say it slowly, carefully, having practised.

Asha would smile, nod. She'd stop using red chilies, but double the green chilies and black pepper.

When Doctorsahib complained about the food, Asha would look crestfallen. "Doctorsahib, you don't like my cooking?"

"No, Asha. No, it is not that, but...."

"So you like my cooking, Doctorsahib? I work hard for you."

"Yes, Asha, I like your cooking, but...."

"*Shukria*, Doctorsahib."

When the food was hot, Doctorsahib didn't eat much. Sometimes there was even enough to take to Sundri's hut. On those days, Tilak didn't grumble so much.

She'd ease off the chilies until Doctorsahib grew relaxed, even complimentary, then slowly increase them again. How it made Doctorsahib run to the toilet! Asha would stand outside, listen to the firecrackers.

Chalak, she was, sly. You had to be in this world. Look at her, free to come and go, and look at Sundri, already big with her third child. Sundri had the same glazed eyes their mother used to have, worrying, worrying, over children.

In Najgulla, begging, it is their mother's fear for them that is hardest to bear.

Some days they fare well, other days they eat out of garbage bins. They sleep where they can, doorways, alleys, the knife always handy. They sleep outside a temple for a while until the *Sadhu* approaches their mother. They need temple prostitutes, young ones, he says, eyeing Sundri and Asha. Her mother, visibly with child, afraid to invite a curse from a *Sadhu*, says, "Forgive us, but not now." They never go back to the temple.

There are so many partition refugees that people are afraid or impatient. It's impossible to get work. The only offers they get are the work for women unaccompanied by men.

And yet, when the very thought is ludicrous, their mother still worries about finding husbands for them, still hopes the baby will be a boy, will miraculously cure their problems.

Occasionally, she talks about returning to Hyderabad, Sindh, which is now in the new Muslim country, Pakistan; she talks about embroidering wall hangings to sell, about meeting their father there. Other times she forgets the happy years in Hyderabad, Sindh, and slips back to the time when they'd left their village because of the drought, the argument they'd had when they'd left – should they go east, past Rajasthan, into Madhya Pradesh, maybe south, to Bombay, or should they go west to Hyderabad, Sindh? Hyderabad, Sindh is closer, but how will the girls find good husbands there, with so many Muslims?

But it is worst for Asha when her mother remembers. Asha cannot bear the look. It's there because of the unborn child and because of them, Sundri and Asha.

❖

Asha hadn't searched Doctorsahib's bureau right away. She suspected a trap. At first, she'd pull open the drawers and look. So strange, the Doctorsahib's clothes, so fine, the material, the stitching. Finer even than the stitching Asha's father used to do. And her underclothes. The *chuddi*, the underpants, had no string, just thread that snapped back when you pulled it. The material was silky, not the rough cotton the villagers wore, those who had underwear.

When Asha took Doctorsahib's clothes to the river, the village women would cluster around, eager to touch. Meenu even smelled Doctorsahib's underpants once.

Asha laughed and shouted, "Hey, Meenu, an English woman's bum smells the same as an Indian's. Want to sniff mine?" How the women roared. From then on they called Meenu "Chuddi."

The women were interested in all the Doctorsahib's Angrezi things. The stick with bristles on it that she used to clean her teeth, no Neem twig for her; the wonderful soap, smooth, that smelled better than flowers; the white liquid Doctorsahib used on her hands. One time Doctorsahib gave Asha some. It made her skin as soft as a petal.

And all the bottles of medicine Doctorsahib had. There was a blue bottle that Doctorsahib always ran for after eating hot food. One time Asha had hidden it. Doctorsahib had been frantic until Asha produced it, claiming to have moved it whilst tidying up.

Asha mimicked Doctorsahib's Hindi, described her habits. So dirty she was, she never washed properly when she went to the toilet, used paper not water. And she ate with her left hand. *Chee*, imagine not knowing the left hand was for cleaning the body, the right one for eating. The women wrinkled their noses, giggled.

Gradually, Asha became more daring. She examined the contents of the bureau drawers, the items underneath, always careful to replace everything exactly as before. That was the only trouble with Doctorsahib, she was too tidy. With a messy Memsahib, it was easier to poke around undetected.

Already her search had been profitable. She'd seen the box with white, rectangular objects in the bottom drawer. Bandages, Asha had thought, until she'd seen Doctorsahib carrying the box into the bathroom, later seen one wrapped in paper, soiled. Imagine using something like that, so smooth, soft.

Asha covered her face, went to Doctorsahib. "Excuse me, Doctorsahib, I don't like to mention it, but...."

"Yes, what is it, Asha?"

Asha lowered her head, whispered, "Do you have any spare rags? It's my time of the month, and I need some more."

Doctorsahib had given her some pads, and even a belt to hold them in place. The next time Doctorsahib had gone to Najgulla she had bought a whole box for Asha, and from then on, every month, Asha was well supplied. She had told Doctorsahib how heavy her blood was. Asha did quite well selling two here, two there for a paisa.

"*Arré*, Asha, you're getting too bold," said Meenu, one day, by the river. "One of these times she'll be onto you and then you'll get into trouble. Big trouble."

"What do you mean, trouble? You watch your mouth, Chuddi. If you say one word to any of the Sahib-log, I'll come after you, pull your hair out by the roots, d'you hear?"

"*Ai-yai-yai.* I'm not going to say anything. I'm just worried about you."

"I can take care of myself, Chuddi. You better watch yourself, I know how that Rohet watches you when you go behind the bushes. Careful you don't get it. Right between the legs."

The women laughed. Asha banged the clothes against the rock. Get into trouble! As if she was so stupid. She could take bits of food,

25

even the odd piece of clothing – it floated down river during the wash, she was so sorry, Doctorsahib could stop the money from her wages. Of course, Doctorsahib never did.

But Asha never took money, except for a few paisa in change when she shopped for food. Doctorsahib kept her money in the top drawer, underneath her underwear. Asha couldn't decide whether the woman was extremely simple or extremely clever. Asha counted the money but never took so much as one rupee. She had no intention of being dismissed from a job which, on the whole, was satisfactory.

❖

It was the morning after the interchange with Chuddi that Asha found the embroidery threads. She'd never noticed them before because they were folded in a long piece of cloth, inside a clear plastic bag. Asha had seen the cloth and ignored it. It looked like a piece of cheap cotton.

That morning she took out the plastic bag, unfolded the fabric. Out fell embroidery threads. Red, orange, pink, peach, every shade of green. On the cloth was printed a pattern of flowers.

Asha sat on the floor, the cloth in her hand. How fine the threads were. In her village the threads had never been like this.

❖

"Asha. Asha, come here now, right now."

Asha ignored her mother. She was happier playing outside or helping her father in the field.

"Asha, come now or I'll give you a beating."

Her father looked at her. "You'd better go, quick, or you'll get it."

Asha ran back to the hut of her parents, her grandparents and her older uncles' families.

Her mother shook her head, clicked her tongue. "What a wild thing you are. Why can't you be like Sundri? See how nicely she's making that *choli?*"

Sundri sat in the shade, hands flying, covering the short blouse with vibrant threads in the geometric pattern distinctive to their family.

Her grandmother said, "Leave the girl alone. She is only five."

"Yes, but she must learn. Get going, Asha, work on your cloth."

Asha pushed her hair off her face, took a small drink of water from the pot in the hut – you had to be careful, it was always short. She pulled out her grimy piece of cloth. *Khhsss!* What a dull, dusty sound the thread made. *Khsss!* In, out, in out.

Her grandmother smiled. "Come. I've got a gift for you."

She opened the worn trunk in the corner of the hut and held out a rag doll, with coarse, dark threads for hair, brown embroidered eyes and a wide, red mouth. "See, you can make clothes for her and embroider them. That will be more fun, yes?"

Asha sighed. How strange to think of Doctorsahib doing embroidery.

At the Ungoli house, Parvati Memsahib had sometimes done simple, flowery patterns, nothing like the bold work in Asha's home village. But Asha could hardly glance at Parvati Memsahib's work, let alone touch the threads.

It was only when they'd still lived in their Kutch village that Asha had disliked the work. It hadn't seemed special then. Every woman in the house did it, every wall hanging, every quilt, every garment they wore was covered with colourful embroidery. But when they left the village because of that drought, Asha missed the colours.

And it was their making in Hyderabad, Sindh. Nasser Aziz, a Muslim tailor, taught her father his trade in exchange for the embroidery Sundri, Asha, and her mother did. Soon, her mother had gold bangles.

Her mother said Asha had a real gift for adapting the village styles, combining them in fresh ways. She'd embroidered clothes for her doll, such beautiful clothes.

Asha's hands shook slightly as she carefully put away the embroidery threads, folded the cloth, and returned it to its plastic bag.

She gathered the dirty clothes and went down to the river.

The women were talking about Ungoli *Burra* Memsahib, how badly she treated her daughter-in-law, Parvati Memsahib, all the work she made her do, and her big with child.

Asha's voice was harsh. "What're you going on about, poor Parvati Memsahib, poor Parvati Memsahib? Poor, my arse! She's rich, isn't she, with wealthy parents? She can go anywhere, do anything. Stupid fool, she's got no spine."

She spread Doctorsahib's towel on the flat rock, scrubbed it with hard soap.

Jaya, a wiry old woman who worked at the Ungoli house, shook her head and clicked her tongue. "Listen to you. You've got no pity for anyone."

Asha pounded the towel against the rock. "Why should I have pity for *Sahib-log*? We're the ones working our guts out. Look at this Doctorsahib now, what I have to put up with, her dirty habits, eating with her left hand, her awful Hindi. She's been here for months and she still can't speak properly. And fussing, fussing, fussing about food, never satisfied. I don't know how much longer I can stand it."

"You'd better watch your tongue, Asha *rani*. You have it cushy at Doctorsahib's, and all you do is abuse her, trick her, cheat her."

Asha hawked and spat into the water. "All of a sudden so pure and lofty? I've heard you many a time abusing Ungoli Memsahib."

"Yes, but Ungoli Memsahib is a different sort. I've been to the clinic. Doctorsahib treated me well."

There was a chorus of agreement from the other women.

"*Chumchas!* Sucking up to the Angrezi-log."

"What's Doctorsahib done to you? She feeds you, pays you well, and look how you treat her. She's all alone, a stranger. You have no heart, no pity."

"You're too old, Jaya. Your brain has dried, sitting out in the sun." Asha banged the towel so hard against the rock she grazed her knuckles.

She gathered the clean clothes and strode back to Doctorsahib's bungalow. In the kitchen she noisily set about preparing Doctorsahib's lunch, chopping up an extra large green chili for the *dahl*.

After the meal, Doctorsahib called Asha, who instantly put on her smile.

Doctorsahib's face was still flushed, her eyes moist. "I will not be in for the evening meal today. I am going to Najgulla and I will be late, so I will eat there."

Asha lowered her head. "Doctorsahib, you don't like my cooking?"

"No, no, Asha." Doctorsahib blinked uncertainly. "It is just that I have to go to Najgulla. I have work to do. So I might as well eat there. That way, you will have a free afternoon."

Asha smiled. "Very good, Doctorsahib."

When Doctorsahib left, Asha ate the leftovers and quickly cleared the dishes.

She walked into the front room, slowly looked around. No evening meal to prepare, and she could iron the clothes tomorrow.

Almost involuntarily, she went into Doctorsahib's bedroom. She knelt in front of the bureau, opened the bottom drawer. She took out the threads.

She hesitated, then pulled a length of the brightest red. The red of the *khameez* of her *gudiya*, her doll.

❖

In the frenzy, Asha grabs her doll.

"We don't have time for that now." Her mother slaps her. "Get something useful."

"Never mind," says her father. "Let the child have something to comfort her." He picks up the kitchen knife.

Asha stands frozen, clutching her doll. Her mother thrusts a bundle at her. She's snatching up clothes, food, pots, hissing orders to Sundri, who also rushes around, gathering things.

Why do they have to go? Why in the middle of the night?

Nasser Uncle is there, helping them load the bullock cart.

"Take the machine," he says, putting the new sewing machine from the shop on the cart. "And here, my wife sends this food. Hurry, you must hurry."

In the warm August night, her father swings her on the cart. Sundri clambers up behind her. Her mother is crying, her mother who is always so strong?

Nasser Uncle reaches up, hugs Sundri and Asha. His mouth shakes, his face is wet. "Allah be with you."

Her mother takes off two of her gold bangles, holds them out to Nasser Uncle.

"No, you will need them. Allah guide you."

Her father embraces Nasser Uncle.

"Go now, my brother. And don't take any trains. There are terrible stories."

At the front of the cart, her father swings the whip, *kaa-thaaa*. They lurch forward. Asha doesn't know why she's so frightened. Maybe it's because everyone else is, she can smell it.

"Shh." Her mother's voice is low and fierce. "A big girl like you, there's no need to cry. You must stop. D'you want to get us all killed?"

"But why are we going, Ma? When will we come back?"

"Shh! I don't know. Don't ask any more questions. Just be quiet." Asha presses her face into her doll. Her mother's hand strokes her head, but her movements are rough, jerky. They frighten Asha into silence.

❖

Asha sprang to her feet, ran to the window. What if it was a trick? What if, right now, Doctorsahib was sneaking back?

No one in sight, no noise, just the steady pulsing of the afternoon sun.

She knelt again by the bureau, fingered the threads. You couldn't do much with one piece of red. She pulled out strands of crimson, fuchsia, emerald. What was a little thread to the Angrezi-log?

❖

The Angrezi-log are leaving the country at last, but they're determined to make Muslims and Hindus fight each other; they have broken the country in two.

Asha doesn't understand. She's seen many Angrezis, but none seem so strong that they can break the land. Do they snap it like a biscuit?

Her mother is angry. Maybe it's just rumours. Half their belongings left behind, a new baby coming, a boy this time, pray God. They've seen no trouble. This is just Nasser Aziz's trick to get their goods.

"Stupid woman," cries her father. "He risked his life to warn us. We're all right so far because we left soon enough. And we're not there yet."

"There, there. Where is this new border, do you know? You're too trusting, and here that Aziz, *sala gandoo,* is laughing with our things."

Asha, jolted, parched, clings to her doll. The world has gone mad.

❖

It was that stupid Doctorsahib's fault. Typical of the Angrezi-log, they never trusted anyone. Hadn't she told Asha, after the midday meal that she would not return until late that evening?

She'd done it on purpose, of course, to catch Asha. Asha had been kneeling by the bottom drawer, trying to decide which colours she could safely take more of, when there she was, Doctorsahib herself, at the door.

"What are you doing?"

Asha had been unable to speak, had felt her eyes filling with tears.

Doctorsahib, her mouth a thin line, had said, "Put it back. I do not have time now. I will talk to you tomorrow. I came back for something I had forgotten."

Asha hadn't had the wit to pretend she hadn't understood or even to invent some excuse, however implausible.

31

She tucked in the last stray end of the mosquito net under the bed. How could she have been so absorbed that she hadn't heard?

Voices wailing, crying, whimpering, shouting. The long stream of carts, people walking, heading from the border area. Both ways, Hindus, Muslims. The terrible things they've seen, heard, the talk. Women weeping, dead bodies by the roadside, naked women, blood between the legs.

Her father keeps the knife handy. Her mother's nose is swollen; the slit where the nose ring was torn off is infected. Her eyes when she looks at Asha and Sundri. So many families have lost their children; some have sold their daughters.

Asha hugs her doll. When they get there, wherever that is, she'll wash her doll's clothes, and everything will be clean, bright.

Down. Her father jumps to the ground, overturns the cart. Her doll, the quilts they have pieced over the years, the ones they are to sell to start again, the sewing machine, bouncing, bursting. Asha screams, can't reach her doll. Her father thrusts them under the cart, pushes it down. It bangs against Asha's head. Cattle bawl.

Screams, her ears are soaked in screams. Her mother calls her father's name, pulls Asha and Sundri close against her, one hand on each of their mouths. Drowning in the thunder of her mother's heart, her familiar smell, her sweat and something else. Sundri must have soiled herself. No, it's her, mess in her pants, stench of fear, her mother wailing. Asha presses her hand against her mother's mouth, presses hard. Cries burst uncontrollably against her palm, snot runs over her hand.

❖

There weren't many clothes to wash; if she was still here tomorrow, she'd do them then, otherwise someone else would inherit the Angrezi woman's stinking clothes. Besides, she didn't want to face the women at the river. Would they guess? They'd find out soon enough. They'd pretend to commiserate, but they'd be delighted. They'd even fight over who was to get her job.

Asha gave the chair in the small front room a last rub. The house was clean, and she'd already cooked the *bhaji,* the hottest ever, three large green chilies. It made even her eyes water. She hawked, spat into the *bhaji.* There, Doctorsahib, a good-by present from Asha.

She didn't need this Angrezi Doctor. She'd go back to the Ungolis. And if she couldn't get on there, she'd go to Najgulla where plenty of families needed servants. She'd never be forced into marriage, have children. Look at Sundri now, so worn.

❖

When her mother's water breaks, two months too soon, no one will take them to the hospital. Asha screams, people ignore her. Just another mad beggar.

Half-pulling, half-carrying, they drag their mother the mile to the hospital.

The gates are shut to keep marauders out. Once a Hindu crowd broke in, killed a Muslim patient and doctor.

Asha shouts to the *chowkidar.* "Hurry up. My mother is having a baby. Hurry."

The small, thin *chowkidar* looks at them and sniffs. He puts finger and thumb on either side of his nose, blows expertly. His snot, greenish-yellow, globular, lands in the dust by Asha's bare foot. Her mother moans, clings to the gate of the hospital, knuckles white.

"Open the gate, you *sala gandoo,*" screams Asha. "Open it, you motherfucker, or I'll cut your dick off."

"Who d'you think you are, you piece of garbage? Get out of here. This is a hospital for decent folk."

"My mother, she's having a baby."

The *chowkidar* swings his stick. "More likely drunk, by the looks of you. Out of the way. Move, or I'll call the police."

He bangs his stick against her mother's fingers, and pokes it through the bars of the gate.

In the distance, Asha sees a white-clad figure.

33

"Doctorsahib," she yells.

Sundri weeps, her nose overflowing, clinging to their mother.

Asha holds onto the gate, eyes closed, shouts, over and over, "Doctorsahib, Doctorsahib."

Her fingers are bloody from the *chowkidar*'s stick before a voice says, "What is this noise?"

Asha looks into the dark, pocked face of a woman in a white coat.

"What's the matter?" she says in a voice that is low yet annoyed.

The *chowkidar* licks his lips, talks fast in a whining tone, but the dark woman stops him.

Her mother's labour is not very long. The doctor with the pocked face delivers their dead baby brother, tries with a nurse and another doctor to stop their mother's bleeding.

Asha stares at her mother. Still. Her awful eyes closed at last. Sundri is at the foot of the bed, sobbing, a heaving bundle of brown rags.

Slowly, Asha picks up, from where it has fallen, the knife her mother had taken from their father's body.

Doctorsahib. Asha carried the food into the front room, put it on the table with a thud.

Doctorsahib sank into the chair, her face red. She fanned herself with the newspaper.

"It is a very hot day, is it not, Asha?"

What was the woman playing at, speaking so politely? Still trying to torment her.

Doctorsahib gulped down a glass of water, looked at her.

Asha's heart beat faster. Tilak would be furious. Would she be able to work for the Ungolis again? Her place had been filled. How would she get a job with no reference? She'd end up back in the streets, babies thrust inside her.

"What were you doing with my things?"

She'd prepared for this. From her waist she pulled the rag on which she'd worked the embroidery.

Doctorsahib frowned.

"What is it?"

34

"A doll's *salwar*. We used to do this kind of embroidery in the village I come from." She hadn't meant to say so much.

"I do not like stealing," said Doctorsahib.

Asha stared back, her face expressionless. This ugly woman, *Burra* Angrezi Sahib, sitting there, wanting to extract penance, like a tooth.

"But since it was not anything...." Doctorsahib hesitated, continued, "... anything serious, I will overlook it this time."

What did she expect, Asha to touch her feet?

"The next time you want something, you ask me. Understand?"

Asha nodded, almost imperceptibly.

"I do not want you to go through my things again, understand? I want to trust you. And I want you to trust me."

Asha stared at the plate of steaming food.

"I also like to do embroidery, but here I do not have the time. My aunt taught me, my mother's sister, in the village I come from, in England." She paused. "If you like, the next time I go to Najgulla, I can get threads for you. As a gift."

What was the woman's game?

Doctorsahib pulled the plate towards her, bit into a piece of *chapati* wrapped around the *bhaji*. She sucked in her breath sharply, her ugly blotches drowning in the flood of colour.

"*Bahaut tikha hai,* so hot." Eyes watering, she said stumblingly, "But I like your cooking."

Asha curved her mouth into a smile. What a fool, this Doctorsahib, a slug with weeping eyes, pathetic.

Doctorsahib blinked rapidly, licked her lips, gathered another mound of food with her left hand.

Asha's smile widened. So many things she could do, worse than chilies in her food, worse than spit.

She couldn't help it, she started to laugh. She laughed and laughed, unable to stop.

Doctorsahib looked at her, puzzled, then she too was smiling, then laughing, helplessly, foolishly.

Asha, bent over double, saw Doctorsahib through streaming eyes. Why was she laughing? Didn't she understand? Didn't she know what could happen? Stupid, stupid woman.

MARKET ANALYSIS

MALA STRODE OVER THE GRASS, oblivious of the dew. By the time she entered class, her feet and sandals were soaked, the bottoms of the legs of her jeans dark with dampness.

The classroom was only half full. Most of the students were teachers upgrading their qualifications in summer school. Mala slid into a seat between Dave and Shirley, her hands still trembling.

Dave nudged her. "Hey, where the heck were you last night?"

Mala managed a small smile.

"Well, we are distant this morning. Have I got B.O. or something?"

"Get a coffee, Dave," said Shirley.

"What d'you mean, 'Get a coffee, Dave?' What's with the orders?"

"Dave, go and get a coffee."

When he was out of earshot, Shirley said flatly, "Your father?"

Mala swallowed. "The usual, only worse."

"Montreal?"

"He doesn't know yet." Mala twisted her long beaded necklace around her finger. Her mother had whispered that morning that she was going to cook his favourite *russgulla*, and talk to him about McGill after dinner. But it took so little to set him off. If she was silent, *Answer me, show some respect.* If she said anything, *Don't you talk back to me. I will not have you acting like those white girls, always being disrespectful.*

"He's sick," she blurted. "I can't do anything right." She stopped. Dave was back with the coffee.

Dave's face was red, his eyes troubled behind his glasses. "Look, if I said anything...."

Mala shook her head. "It's okay, Dave. It's not you. Family problems." Dave couldn't possibly understand. Shirley knew more than anyone else. But not everything.

Dr. Vernot entered the room, and the Advanced French class began.

Shirley whispered, "I'm going to skip language lab today. Mom's sick. You'll come by later?"

Mala nodded. "Yeah, but I'll be a bit longer than usual. I promised Dave I'd run through some extra tapes with him."

Dave rubbed his ears and slumped back in his chair. "Don't know how you do it, wrapping your tongue around those words."

"It's easy."

"Well, you're some good at it."

"Yeah, but there are no third- or fourth-year classes."

"So, go somewhere else."

"Go somewhere else!" She gave a bark-like laugh.

"What's the big deal?"

Mala glanced uncertainly at him. "My father – " How could she even start to explain the constant watching, the suspicions, the curfews? She'd always tried to minimize the difference between herself and her friends.

Dave's Adam's apple bobbed up and down. "Hey, you're nineteen. He can't stop you. Tell him to fuck off."

"Great, Dave. D'you tell your father to fuck off?"

Dave ran his hands through his hair.

"Come on, let's go. Can you drop me off at Shirl's?"

"What's the hurry? Why don't we grab a bite first, someplace downtown?"

"I don't know." If her father saw her with Dave....

"Come on. Can't you have lunch with a friend?"

Mala hesitated. "Okay, but you'll have to drop me off at Shirley's

38

right after." She'd told her father she'd be there studying. He always called to check.

"Where to?" asked Dave, as they got into his sputtering Pinto.

"McDonald's." Her father wouldn't be caught dead near beef.

❖

Mala glanced at her watch. Still plenty of time before her 5.00 PM curfew. She picked up two pencils, drummed them against the table.

Shirley stared at a pair of flies noisily mating on the kitchen window sill. "Know what?"

"What?"

"Dave's got a thing about you."

Mala's hands froze. "What d'you mean, thing? Like what?"

"Like crush."

"Dave! Don't be silly. What about Elaine?"

"She won't even look at him. D'you ever notice that about Dave? Always hankering after girls he can't have? The princess-in-the-tower bit."

"So?"

"So, that's how he looked at you. Today."

"Oh, come on! We've known each other forever. I mean, he's nice and all, but.... Thanks a lot, Shirl."

They burst out laughing. Mala resumed her tattoo.

But Rob Putnam, now that was something different. He was tall, blond, and he'd liked her, too, just her, Mala. No small miracle that. There were guys who'd never go out with her because of her colour and others who wanted to because of it, anticipating an exoticism she didn't have. Rob, he'd just liked her, asked her out.

Shirley said she should have gone, she should have lied to her father. Anyway, Rob hadn't broken his heart over it.

What would it be like, having a boyfriend, sleeping with him? Fantasies. There wasn't one other girl she knew who didn't have some kind of relationship. She hated being around them when they swapped stories.

"Hard at work?" Shirley's mother, in a blue bathrobe, her wiry grey hair disarrayed, shuffled into the kitchen.

39

"Oh, hi, Mrs. Nealy."

"Feeling better?" Shirley asked.

"My head aches, my throat's sore, I'm all stuffed up, and I ache all over."

"Poor little Mom. I suppose that's your way of saying you want me to make supper?"

Mrs. Nealy grinned. "You're a good kid, Shirl."

Mala looked out the window. *A good kid.* Simple words.

"Mala, have you sent your application to McGill?" Mrs. Nealy asked.

"No. Not yet. There's no point getting my hopes up. My father'll never let me go."

"Well, if he's worried about your accommodation, I can give you my cousin Miriam's address in Montreal. She boards students. Actually, if you want, I can call your father and vouch for her."

"Thanks, Mrs. Nealy, but not yet. He doesn't know about McGill." Somehow she couldn't tell Mrs. Nealy that today was the day her mother was cooking all his favourite food.

"Why wouldn't he let you go?" Mrs. Nealy's forehead creased slightly.

"Because he's determined to keep me under him." The words blurted out.

There was a long silence, then, "Shirley, be a dear and get my slippers from upstairs."

As soon as Shirley left the kitchen, Mrs. Nealy said, "Mala, what's happening at home?"

Mala looked down and pushed back a cuticle.

Mrs. Nealy spoke slowly, carefully, "Mala, is he doing anything? Is there anything. . . ." Her voice trailed away.

It took a few seconds to register. Mala looked up, shocked. "Oh no, it's nothing like that. I mean he's a bastard, but he'd never do anything like that."

Mrs. Nealy patted her hand. "I'm sorry. I didn't mean to imply. . . . But if you ever need to talk, I'm here."

Mala stared at Mrs. Nealy, at the flakes of skin peeling around her reddened nostrils. She'd known Mrs. Nealy for years, but that didn't give her the right to pry, to insinuate.

As Shirley came back with the slippers, the kitchen clock struck five.

"Is that the right time? Five o'clock?" Mala tapped her watch. "Oh my God, my watch's stopped. He'll kill me." Of all the days to be late.

She tucked the books under her arm, walking swiftly, shaken by the ugliness of Mrs. Nealy's suspicion. Was it possible that Mrs. Nealy thought *those* people did ugly, horrible things? For an instant, Mala's childhood affection for her father rushed to his defense. He may be paranoid and tyrannical but he'd never . . . do that.

Horns blared behind her. A large white car with pink and blue streamers, followed by other cars, honked past. June was polluted with weddings. She caught a glimpse of a white-clad figure in the first car. There weren't many virgin brides nowadays. In India they wore red. Virginity was prized, essential. Red for rejoicing, red for the blood of a virgin, white for mourning.

The only Indian wedding she remembered was her Auntie Rekha's in Barundabad, just before they'd come to Canada. Mala had been eight. A jumble of bright lights, music, food, flowers, laughter, and a beautiful bride glittering in magenta silk and jewels.

One of Mala's great-aunts, Shobha, an insatiable matchmaker, loudly teased a young man, Pradeep, about finding him a girl. Strange that Mala remembered his name, even how he looked: medium height, loose mouth, bristly mustache. Shobha caught her up in a hug. "Your turn will come soon enough, Mala. We'll have no trouble marrying you off, a fair girl like you. And we'll find you a good-looking, fair boy, just like that Pradeep –" She stopped abruptly as she saw Mala's father approaching, and added hastily, "Not that it matters how a boy looks, as long as he's clever and well off."

Mala hadn't understood her father's anger then. Dazzled by the image of herself as the bride, she'd said, "When I grow up, I want to have a big wedding just like Auntie Rekha's."

Stupid kid. Mala broke into a run, for once oblivious of the sea, glistening in the distance. When she'd been little, in Bombay, her father had laughed more, and occasionally spoiled her, taking her to Chowpatti or the Hanging Gardens. Her lips tightened at the thought of him, watching the clock, fuming. That was another life.

"Tell him to fuck off," Dave had said.

She whispered it, said it aloud, "Fuck off. Fuck off, Dad!" The power of the word, the sharp, stinging sound.

As she neared the house, her father twitched aside the living-room sheers. Her stomach sank. Her hand was sweaty around the doorknob, her chest heaving. The familiar fragrance of Indian spices engulfed her as she opened the door.

"Why you are late? What have you been up to? You were told to be home at five and look at the time now."

"I'm sorry." Mala made her voice meek. "My watch stopped and I didn't notice the time."

"Your watch stopped. Your watch stopped. And I suppose they are having no clocks in your friend's house?"

"I'm sorry." She mustn't make it worse. Not today.

"You're sorry. Always you're sorry but never you're on time. What are you up to that you never notice the time? Who else was there to make – "

"Mala." Her mother's voice. "Come and give me a hand."

Reprieve.

"Go," snapped her father. "Go and help."

Her mother was frying something at the stove.

"You have to be more careful of the time, Mala. Your daddy gets worried."

Mala bit back a retort and kissed her mother, her quiet mother who usually intervened in time. On the counter was a bowl of *russgulla*.

"Oooh, can I have one?" Mala reached towards the bowl of creamy dumplings in syrup. Her mother gently dashed her hand away.

"Later. Go on up and wash nicely. Dinner is almost ready. Then you can come down and take these *pakoras* to your daddy."

Mala put her arms around her mother. "Thanks, Mom. Let's hope the *pakoras* are good." She giggled nervously.

Her mother kissed her cheek and patted it. "I am not promising anything. Your daddy is not going to be keen on this McGill idea. It was difficult enough talking him into letting you take a university degree in the first place." Her voice grew forced. "He is only wanting your good, to see you safely married to a nice boy, if you will only think...."

Mala let go her mother's waist. "I'm going to wash."

When she came back into the kitchen, her father was talking.

"What were you thinking of, Parvati? Nobody is wanting shoddy goods."

"I'm sorry, Mohan. It was a bargain, seventy-five percent off, a bankruptcy sale."

Then Mala saw the flat rectangular package in his hand. Bed linen.

Her father opened the package, shook out a white sheet. "Look at this. Thin, cheap, cotton, bumps in the weave. Who is wanting to buy stuff like that? No wonder the shop went bankrupt." He clicked his tongue. "When we first came here, *Made in Canada* meant something. Now it is only junk. Throw it out, Parvati."

"But, Mohan, what waste. At least – "

"The waste is buying stuff like that, Parvati. We have money for first-class merchandise. Throw it out. I don't want rubbish in my house."

"All right, Mohan, go and get your drink. Mala will bring you some *pakoras*."

Mala set the plate in front of her father, returned to the kitchen, and folded the sheet her father had flung on the floor.

"Tell Sunil and Arun to wash up for dinner," said her mother.

The *pakoras* were good. Her father's good humour soared with the meal, peaked when he saw the *russgulla*. He laughed with the boys as they argued about who was better at ping-pong.

He pushed his chair from the table, loosened his belt, leaned back, hands behind his head, and crossed his legs. "That was a real feast,

Parvati. See, Mala, you must learn to cook like that if you want to keep your husband happy."

"Why don't you take your coffee to the deck? I'll do the dishes." Her mother smiled.

As Mala loaded the dishwasher, she saw her father relaxing in a lawn chair, while her mother poured the coffee.

As soon as the kitchen was tidy, Mala ran upstairs and locked herself in the bathroom. The window, slightly ajar, was directly above the deck. Her father's and mother's voices floated up in the calm June air.

Mala lowered the toilet seat cover, kneeled on it, and leaned towards the window. She lifted her long hair off her sweating neck, pulling at the strands entangled in the black beads of her necklace.

"Her teacher says she should go. She is having a real talent for French and she is wanting to major in it. You know she can't do that here."

A cup rattling against a saucer, then her father's voice, raised. "I am surprised at you, Parvati, taking that girl's nonsense and turning against my wishes."

"Oh, no, Mohan, you know I would never do that, *kabi nahi.*"

"Then what are you are plotting with her?"

"Mohan, no one is plotting. I am only mentioning –"

"Mentioning, my foot. You want her to be like the girls here? All they are talking about is sex, sex, sex! If she is going to Montreal, what will she get up to? *Pagal hai, ladki,* she is young and silly and totally unreliable. She could not even be on time today."

"But, Mohan, she is mostly on time, and today she was only fifteen minutes late."

"So, you are encouraging this nonsense. Wonderful. McGill! God knows what that girl will get up to. Ruin herself. Is that what you want for your daughter? So no decent boy will want her?"

"Mohan, you know she is a sensible girl, *bahaut sharif ladki hai,* she is not going with boys or doing anything bad."

"Only because I am here to watch her. Montreal! You want her running around with boys, like that Amrita Shankar? I don't know what the matter is with the Shankars, letting their daughter behave

44

like that. They are completely gone mad with Western ways." His voice flamed with fury.

"Mohan, we have been living here since she was little. All her friends are Canadian, she – "

"Her friends, her friends. I don't want to hear about her friends. They are the problem. Teaching her to look down on us." His voice rose to a shriek. "What is Mala thinking? She should be going out with white boys? Does she think she is too good for a *kala admi*?"

There was a long silence. Mala leaned her head against the window sill. *Kala admi*, black man. She picked at a grimy, dark fuzz ingrained in the corner of the window frame. Mould. It was too deep.

"Don't be looking at me like that now, Parvati. I should never have let you talk me into putting off her marriage, let her go to university. French will not improve her value as a bride. She should have gone into Domestic Science, like you. All these big ideas she is getting, mixing with her fancy friends. Finished. First thing tomorrow I will write to my brothers' families, tell their wives to start looking around right away for a good boy."

"Mohan, she is still only young – "

"No, my mind is made up. This McGill idea just shows the sooner she is married the better. Meantime, she only goes to class then straight home. No friends, nothing. You have been too easy on her, spoiling her...."

There was a rapping on the bathroom door. Sunil growled, "Hurry up, Mala. What're you doing, flushing yourself down?"

Silently, Mala closed the window and opened the door.

"Jeez, you took long enough."

In her room, Mala shut the door, sank into bed. Her face stung, as though she'd been slapped. She should have known McGill would only make things worse. She should've thought, her mother should've realized.

The thought crept in, mushroomed. Maybe her mother had realized. Maybe this was her way of pushing her into it.

She buried her face against the bedcover, elaborately embroidered, fuchsia, with tiny mirrors sewn into it. She flung it on the floor. Pink, huddled like hastily discarded clothes, mirrors winking like jewels. Mala fell on her bed and lay still until her stomach stopped rocking.

The day after Auntie Rekha's wedding. No wonder she remembered her father's cousin Pradeep. It was him she'd seen the next morning. Behind her grandmother's bungalow, outside the courtyard, Pradeep, partially behind a bush. In his hand was something hard, dark. He was rubbing it back and forth, face twisted. He'd looked up, then turned towards her, rubbing harder. His face had been contorted with something she couldn't name. And with rage.

Rekha, weighted with silk and jewels, queen of the day. What came after? Is that what they wanted for her? Her legs wrenched apart like a dead cow in a slaughterhouse?

Her mother. What had it been like for her? Had she met him before, felt anything for him? What had it been like for her mother, the wedding night? Her gentle, beautiful mother.

Her mother never mentioned sex.

When the sobs ceased, she scrambled under the blankets, arms around her knees. No spoilt goods, no seconds, nothing damaged. She laughed, stopped, mustn't get hysterical.

Why was he so obsessed with controlling her? Wasn't it enough that he'd had her mother? Why must he pick who she fucked?

An image flashed in her mind, of her lying flat on a marriage bed, on top of her a faceless husband. And on top of her husband, shoving him hard, hard, harder into her, her father, his face distorted with rage. And lust. Like Pradeep.

She sat bolt upright. She must be going crazy. Mrs. Nealy had got to her, that was it.

Arranged marriage, tradition, pick and choose. She twirled her necklace until it tightened around her neck. Not that there was much choice here. There were guys who'd never date her. They weren't the type who hissed, "Paki!" in the street, just always saw her kind as strangers. But they'd fuck a stranger. In the end, no different from someone her father picked.

Many years since she hadn't been afraid of him, many. Poisonous little man, dark, homely, tyrannical. Damaged. Damaged goods, reduced. Unmarketable.

She dragged her necklace off. Strands of tiny Rajasthani beads twisted together, unvarying as a genetic code.

Tomorrow. Her father would have to let her go to class. She'd wait outside for Dave, they'd skip class, drive some place quiet.

She twisted the necklace hard. It burst, the cord biting into her skin. In all her fantasies, it had never been Dave, never. But at least he wasn't a stranger.

MUNI

I CANNOT SIT HERE ANY LONGER, pretending to watch television. Mohan also is not watching, even though his eyes are never leaving the screen. I can tell from the way he is sitting, all straight, arms crossed, the way his nose and eyes are twitching.

The house is silent as if there has been a death.

"Where you are going?" he says sharply. He is still looking at the television.

"To the *puja ka kamara.*" I know he will not stop me going to my prayer room.

"You are not to speak to her. You understand? I forbid it."

"Mohan, what is the sense – "

"*Bilkul nahi,* not one word. Always you are spoiling her. Now see what's happened?"

"I am going to do my *puja* now."

"Yes, and you'd better pray God knocks some shame into her."

Today I feel old. It is fashion to say thirties and forties are best years, but my legs ache, I get out of breath walking upstairs.

Silence is louder up here. The boys are in the basement. They know to keep out of the way.

Her room is locked. Mohan has the key in his pocket. I push my gold bangles tightly up my arm so they will not tinkle. From outside her door, not a sound, not even of weeping. Gently, I touch the door, as I used to smooth her cheek when she was only little. *Sub chup hai,* still quiet.

I go to my room, open the door to my *puja ka kamara.* It is supposed to be a walk-in closet, but what use do I have for a walk-in

49

closet if I do not have a prayer room? Always, since my marriage, in my *puja ka kamara* I find comfort and peace.

I turn on the light, cover my head with my sari, sit in front of the low table holding the Ramayana and Bhagavad Gita. They are covered with a brocade cloth. On the wall ahead are pictures of Vishnu, Lakshmi, Rama, Krishna.

I light *agarbatti,* the incense. Always, I have been careful about fire. I bring my hands together. They are shaking. I will read aloud from the Gita. It will help compose my mind. My voice cracks.

The smoke rising from the *agarbatti* curls towards me, calming, like thin ice over churning water.

Vishnu, guide me. Help me find strength to do my duty. *Hai Bhagwan,* what she has done is bad, very bad, but she is my *muni,* I long to comfort her. *Sach hai,* she was influenced by her friends. Girls in Canada are only talking about love, love, like it is only thing that matters. Security is what really matters. When they are getting to my time of life, they will understand.

Mohan is right to want to arrange marriage for her, but she will not hear of it. Bad enough refusing to obey him, but sleeping with a boy. A white boy. She told Mohan, taunted him.

Such things, can they run in the blood? My daughter, all mine, not Mohan's. The other man, her father – I cannot call him my lover, even though she was conceived in love. No, I will not think of him, I will vomit blood.

I hear loud laughter from the television downstairs. I do not hear Mohan laughing.

I close my eyes and try to shut out the noise.

If only my mind was working.... What is best to do? I must obey my husband, it is duty. But for me it is more. When I married Mohan, I prayed to Vishnu, Vishnu the Preserver, to save my baby and me. If he spared us, I would never let my husband regret marrying me, be the best Hindu wife, always obey my husband, make him happy. I made that oath, I made it freely. I had learned by then only old ways are best. Useless to try to change karma.

Vishnu spared us both. Always I kept my oath, always I will. Maybe it will make up for some of my sin.

But how she looked at me when he locked her in. She said nothing, but her eyes begged. She is my *muni*. It was for her sake I wanted to live. From first time I felt her stir inside me like butterfly wings, I wanted to live.

She is young, naive. She is not understanding these matters. These love matches also are not always working. Look at the divorce rate. Parents are knowing best for children, checking into background of families children will marry. So many things – security, health, morals, prospects, looks, horoscopes.

It is not so awful. Mohan and I, we are content. I had silly romantic ideas, but we must stick to traditions. No, it has not been bad with Mohan. There are adjustments, yes, but every woman is having to adjust, it is the way. Mohan is no different from other men, not perfect, but look how he provides. She must learn, just as I did.

So much easier, when they are little. When she was tiny, she used to cry for me, her little hands tight, tight, tears rushing down the side of her face. And when I picked her up, put her to my breast, she would grunt, suck. So greedy. She and I, such peace, her mouth moving up and down, tugging my breast. Such content, touching her cheek, knowing only I could satisfy her.

Not always I have been able to comfort her. That time, sixteen she was, those white boys, taunting. She tried to laugh. But I saw her pain, her mouth all thin, her eyes like a lid come down. I wanted to hold her, stroke the back of her neck like I used to when she was a baby. How many times there were things said of which I knew nothing?

Motherhood. So much delight, yet so much fear, pain. My mother, did she also struggle between her love for me, *ma ki pyaar,* and her duty?

Young, so young I was. Shaking. White sari, hands shaking. Praying in *puja ka kamara*. Vishnu, grant me strength. Praying for Sati to enter, no pain. Praying. *Hai Ram,* those dark stairs, creeping down. No noise. Alone. In kitchen, my heart, how they did not hear? Enough. No pain. Striking match, one time, two times, three times. The match, at last. Flame under *karahi*. Only way. Honour or shame. Pray. So soon, smoking already, the oil, smell pressing. So soon, dark. Now. Reaching for *karahi*. That scream, I could not help it, how could I? Arm against *karahi*. No pain, all lies. Such throbbing.

How she heard, my mother? So many years since she listened for baby's cry. Ma. Blaze of light. Cockroaches running into cracks.

The *agarbatti* tilts, scented smoke bending crooked. I straighten it.

My poor mother. What she must have gone through. Lifting me, holding me, weeping with my degradation. Wiping my tears, pressing my mouth hard, fingers shaking, wet with sweat, my tears, shaking. *Chup, beti, chup.* She would find a way, I must never, never. Promise her. How fast her breath, so pale her cheeks, her eyes big, big, like I slapped her. Still I hurt for her.

Mohan. She remembered. Always he was wanting me.

The astrologer. Came back pulling her sari tight over her head. That long, heavy, gold necklace, part of her dowry. Astrologer told Mohan's parents only immediate marriage was auspicious, otherwise stars were unfavourable.

Married. In two weeks.

All those treasures she sold. All for my dowry. Everything, not to bring down my mother-in-law's wrath on my head. There, only, she did not succeed.

Those early days in Mohan's home, in Barundabad. Such tricks my mind played, frightening thoughts. Deep wells in Barundabad. Cool, deep, still. No burning. But my mother. Already she had suffered, grown old so suddenly. That only stopped me. Then the flutter and stirring inside me.

Mohan's mother, how she worked me. Like a *ghodi*, a horse. So many servants, still she worked me, found fault. What could I do? Her duty to train me, mine to obey, learn. And at night, my husband.

All that time, afraid. So afraid for when my time came. Praying and praying for my baby to be late. *Bhagwan ka daya,* must have been her karma and mine to live; late, so only a month early. And small baby. Thank God for Dr. Bridget. Putting on her *Burra* Angrezi Doctorsahib voice, telling my mother-in-law, "It's because you've worked her like a horse the baby came early. You can be thankful she's young and strong or both she and the baby would have died."

My baby. Such joy. Mohan also was taking more care. Not his fault. He was not meaning to be unkind. Never violent. And not necessary for a woman to be having pleasure in bed, no matter what these young girls are thinking nowadays. That time I had pleasure – insanity.

My daughter. What was it like for her? Was there gentleness, love? These things only a mother can care about. It binds all women together, the bed.

In India, on wedding night, they decorate bed with flowers – marigold, roses, garlands of jasmine, so white, *kitni khushboo*, so sweet-smelling.

Always, Mohan was wanting to marry me. So beautiful, I was, everybody said. Mohan, short, thin, dark, even with family's wealth he was not attracting many girls. But in a man these things are not important. Look how comfortable we are, so much jewelry he is buying me.

Why I am remembering wedding night now? He took me as is his duty. Hurt only because I was scared. Long after he was sleeping, I did what my mother told me. Jabbed finger with hairpin. Seven times. In the morning, my husband, my mother-in-law, they saw blood on sheet and were satisfied.

How often he was wanting me those first few months. Until my belly grew big, many times ordering me to our room, even in the middle of the day. At least he never took long. And he never expected any carrying on like they are doing on television, so bold.

Mohan is calling down to boys to go to bed. It is late. For once they come immediately. Mohan is locking up, coming upstairs. I do not hear him checking smoke detector. Sometimes he forgets if I do not remind him. Already, the boys are quiet. For the first time they do not look for me to say good-night.

Rustling sounds. Mohan is changing into his *kurta pyjama*. I close my eyes. I must be still. I cannot even repeat one simple prayer.

Mind is muddy, roaring like river in spring. Strange, all my thoughts about early days with Mohan, what good it is doing now? It is my daughter I must think of, what is best. Vishnu, guide me.

"Come to bed now, Parvati," my husband calls. "You have done enough *puja* for that ungrateful girl."

I obey. The *agarbatti* is almost all burnt, ash falling over. Looks like burnt skin shed by snake. Carefully, I put it out.

In bed, Mohan lifts my nightgown. He is still angry, a bit rough. I lie still until he is finished. I think of my daughter.

It is hard for her. She has Canadian friends, goes to Canadian university. Does not understand our ways, almost like a stranger sometimes. Never speaks our language. When I say something in Hindi, she is looking ashamed, always answering in English. She does not want to learn Indian cooking, never wears saris, never even *salwar khameez,* or *bindi.* For years I have saved my good saris for her marriage, nice temple saris, thick, old silk. When I hear her foreign voice, I wonder if she is really baby I sang Hindi lullabies to. *Chanda Mama,* I would sing to her.

Now she is all grown-up, so big, beautiful, so grand. Sometimes she is impatient with me. The way she looks at Mohan. What she is afraid of? Mohan is good man, even if his temper is a little hot. I know how to calm him. A girl should be respecting her father, even fearing him a little, but not like that. Sometimes I think she hates him. Did she learn it from my body, my thoughts? *Hai Ram* – another of my sins?

Mohan is fast asleep now, I can tell by the sound of his breathing, soft, smooth.

It is not easy to picture her in a man's bed, spreading her legs. She must have been willing.

My wedding night with Mohan. After he finished, I turned, lifted arm to cover face. Only then I noticed burn on my arm from *karahi.* All scraped to one side the skin, black, all wet, crumpled. Underneath, red. When he crushed me on flowers, I felt something shift, tear, nothing else. But when I saw burn weeping thick, thick fluid, then I felt it sting. I blew on it, blew on it, but still it hurt. More than the feel of his hands on my legs, my breasts. Slowly, with my finger-nail, I scraped skin, flicked it on top of flowers spilling from bed. How sweet the jasmine smelled, piercing; so hot, musky, the roses.

Moonlight is shining through the window. Such a beautiful, calm night. Mohan's pants are hanging on bedpost. I forgot to put them away. The room is full of shadows. Something on my arm, a long curving mark. No, no, I am imagining. Took time but that scar healed years ago.

I say a silent prayer to Vishnu, push my gold bangles up my arm, tightly. Slowly, slowly, I creep out of bed.

For years I have been saving money, hiding it in *puja ka kamara*. Thought to surprise Mohan one day. I know exactly how much there is, $1232. I take out the money folded under the brocade, under the Gita.

I creep to her room, my thighs sticky with my husband's mois-ture. I touch the door gently, lean my forehead against it, close my eyes. I feel the velvet of the back of her neck, smell soft milky breath. I will not disobey my husband. He forbade me to speak to her. I bend down, slide money under the door. Slowly, quietly, I turn the key. Footsteps, she is coming.

I run back. I put the key in his pocket, slip under the covers of my husband's bed.

A breeze is blowing through the window. What fragrance it brings. Jasmine. No, mock-orange flowers. I myself planted the shrub, yes, that first year in the house. Brides here, I am told, like to wear them. I pray God to look after my *muni*.

Tomorrow I will make all his favourite food. I will soothe him, calm him, make him happy. As always. Maybe it will atone a little. The rest, I am willing to pay for in my next life.

DAFFODILS

THIS TIME OF YEAR, my eye craves colour, bright, glowing yellows, reds. I go to the flower market where there are buckets of daffodils and tulips, and I gaze and gaze until the colours soak into every pore and I'm satiated.

Today, I have an excuse to buy daffodils. Shirley's coming. I haven't seen her in three years. We've written and talked briefly on the phone, but it isn't the same.

I fill an old goldfish bowl with water and arrange the daffodils in it. Six daffodils. As soon as I get a job, I'll buy an armful. The room looks nice, though. It's a sunny day and the windows gleam. I stand still, savour the peace, the order.

Footsteps coming upstairs. I rush out. Shirley drops the huge bag she's carrying. We're hugging and laughing, talking at the same time. We exclaim at how we've changed, touch each other's hair. I show her around my room. She admires the nooks. Says it's almost an apartment.

We flop on the sagging couch. Shirley's full of questions about guys I'm seeing. I tell her about Jean-Marc, who was great in bed but not much good anywhere else, and hint at casual lovers. Actually, it's been a while; the last one was Brad, who said the morning after how he loved dark girls, really he did.

I tell her about the job interviews I've had, my hopes to land a translating job in a big company with branches in Toronto, Vancouver, and London, England.

We talk for over an hour without mentioning Prince Edward

Island at all. I don't want to – that life's over – but I have to ask about Hannah.

"Mom's great. She sends her love."

There's an awkward pause. She's waiting but I won't ask. Anyone I care about writes to me. My brothers write to me.

"Oh, presents, I forgot." Shirley heaves herself out of the couch. A spring rattles and I sink farther into my end.

Shirley drags her suitcase over and takes out a small pink striped bag, the kind you buy fancy soaps or candy in.

"Close your eyes and put your hand in."

"What is it?"

"Just do it."

Hard, smooth curves. I open my eyes, look into the bag. It's full of moon snail shells.

After the long winter we'd walk down to the beach, waiting each day for the ice to break. How my eye used to hunger for that first glimpse of blue.

I pick out the largest shell and hold it to my ear. The hushed roar brings back those early morning walks around our neighbourhood. I didn't always go with Shirley. Not in the mornings, she preferred the afternoons. Yet when I think of the beach, I remember the mornings.

Shirley takes out a sweater she's knitted me, royal blue. As I finger it, try it on, she puts something else on the crate in front of the couch.

"And here're some *pedas* for you," she says in a bright voice.

I freeze. Even without looking directly, I see a small Tupperware box and beside it a rectangular envelope.

"Thanks for the sweater. It's gorgeous, I didn't know you could knit like this."

"Mala." Her voice is quiet.

"Well, what the shit d'you expect? Three years and not one word and now I'm supposed to be thrilled?"

"Come on, she's your mother."

"Some mother. She was going to marry me off. She knew how I felt, damn it." I stare out the window. The roar of traffic is muffled. I always keep the window shut.

Shirley says, "It wasn't her. It was your father."

"She went along with it. And I haven't heard a word in three years. Not one."

"You know she couldn't do anything openly. She still cares. She always asks about you."

"Who the fuck's side are you on, anyway?"

Shirley looks at me in that reasonable way she has, like she's explaining something to a kid. "It's not a question of sides. I've talked to your mom. I know what she's feeling. She –"

"I don't need you to tell me what she feels or thinks." I want to smash Shirley's face. I sit on the hard chair by the window, my hands under me.

"Look." My voice is harsh. "I have two brothers who've managed to keep in touch. I have friends, you. I have me. It's enough."

Shirley shakes her head. Two days, she's going to be here, my best friend. Saddled with old baggage.

We spend the day catching up. We talk fast, no awkward pauses. I don't touch what she's left on the crate, but I see it, a Tupperware box and a silent letter screaming at me.

I cook coq au vin for dinner on the burner in the corner of the room.

"Sorry there's no dessert."

Shirley looks at me, then pointedly at the box on the crate.

I curl my lip. "Help yourself."

Shirley brings the box to the table, opens it, takes a *peda*. I drum my fingers on the table and stare fixedly at the daffodils. They don't even fill the bowl. The box is crammed with yellowish moons, each dented in the centre with a sprinkle of pistachio.

I have a sudden image of my mother in her kitchen, the stray end of her red-and-green sari tucked in at her waist as she mixes and kneads the *khoa* with the sugar and saffron.

"Take a little less, Mala," she says, removing some of the creamy mixture from my hand. She shows me how to shape the *peda* and dent it with my forefinger.

59

"See, you make it sweeter by leaving your fingerprint. You fill it with love." She hugs me, presses her finger into a *peda,* and pops it into my mouth.

We've been in this country only six months and I'm just turning nine. I'm settling into school. Life isn't so strange anymore, but I miss Bombay and all my friends. I don't miss the noise of India, the blaring commotion. It's filthy, disorganized. But I miss the colour, the vendors in Chowpatti, the smell of *chaat, bhelpuri,* the mounds of silver covered *paan.* And the sweet shops, the *burfi, jallebie, luddoo.* Halifax seems so grey, lifeless. There are no Indian sweet shops here.

When I ask for *pedas* for my birthday, Mom says, "I'll manage somehow."

I used to love to stay in the kitchen with her. There were so many strange things outside the home, I clung to the familiar, the aroma of Indian spices, my mother bright in her saris, her gold bangles tinkling as she stirred the milk for the *khoa,* around and around, then with a quick series of scrapes across the centre of the pot.

"Mmm. Good." Shirley takes another.

I start clearing the table. I clear everything except the box. She's left the lid off. I wipe the table around the box. Shirley presses the cover back on and wipes under it.

❖

It's past 2:00 when Shirley and I hit the sack. I take the biggest shell, almost the size of my palm, into the alcove I call my bedroom, slip into bed. I hold the shell to my ear.

In Bombay we had a flat on Marine Drive. Mom and I, we'd wake early, walk down to Nariman Point. Those tiny white jasmine flowers she'd throw in the water as the sun rose, her hands fragrant with their scent.

In Canada, we lived in Halifax at first, in a suburb miles from the sea. Sometimes Mom and I would get up early, stroll down quiet tree-lined streets. It wasn't the same.

Then we moved to P.E.I., bought the house near the strait. The morning walks were best. Mom was always at her prayers by dawn, and if I got up, too, we'd walk together. The houses, so strange with curtains and blinds drawn. Early morning hush, the world belonged to us. In the spring, birds chirping, the first tinge of warmth in the air, blue peeping through grey ice like crocuses. Mom looked so happy.

I remember one evening walk. Our first spring in P.E.I., I missed my Halifax friends. It was hard going to a new school.

When I came home, Mom asked how my day was. I was too big to sit on her knee, but I clung, cried. She didn't say anything, just stroked my hair until I was calm. I told her about Barb's birthday, that I wasn't invited.

I didn't tell her Barb had invited me, then giggled, *I hope I'll understand your mother when she drops you off, she talks funny.*

I'd torn up the invitation, flung it in Barb's face, spat at her, *I don't want to go to your dumb party, you're a jerk.* I hated her, hated my mother for being different, loved my mother. I wanted to punch Barb, rush home and rock my mother. Most of all, I hated myself for the times I looked away when people stared at Mom in her sari, the times I cringed when I heard her accent in public.

When I quieted down, Mom said, "Never mind, there are lots of parties, and when it is your birthday, you can invite who you want."

I never invited many kids. Only the ones who didn't stare or giggle behind their hands.

That evening Mom insisted we go for a walk. We scrambled down to the beach, picked shells, watched the sunset. I found a particularly large moon snail shell. Kept it on my window ledge. Wonder if it's still there.

I roll over, straighten my twisted nightshirt. So she asks after me. Big deal. I graduate and I get *pedas*. Whoopee! Not one letter in three years, not the tiniest recognition I'm alive. Sunil and Arun managed – they wrote – and I kept in touch through Shirley.

How did she get the *pedas* out of the house without my father knowing? Must have taken them to Shirley's house during the day when he was at work. Well, stuff it. I left that life the night I left the house.

She turned away, slipped money under the door, must have been her. Not one word, not even a look, just money shrieking, *Get out of my house.*

Shoving clothes in backpack. Underpants, bras, T-shirts, socks. I felt cramps, something wet. I didn't know what to do with my stained underwear, scrunched it in my backpack. I had only one pad. In the taxi, all the way to the airport, I sat on edge, afraid of a stain more than anything else.

I turn over and sigh. I've managed. More than managed, I've done well. B.A. honours, near the top of my class. I worked, won scholarships. I'm going to get a good job, travel. I have friends, Shirley, Hannah, Miriam. I have my brothers who care.

Those first months at Miriam's, I thought she might contact Shirley, find where I was, write. She couldn't risk anything unexplained on the telephone bill, but she could have written, as Sunil and Arun did.

Eight months after I left, Sunil's letter telling me she had pneumonia. I almost called. But he might be home.

I started to write to her, never sent it. I wanted to write loving words, but my pen pierced the paper. *How could you send me to a strange man's bed to be raped on my wedding night.* I wanted to snap that gold chain off her neck, rip those saris she was saving for my wedding, tell her, get better, take care, stay well, drop dead, I don't care.

I close my eyes tightly. I must sleep. So many things to tell Shirley, so much more to show her. If only she'll stop digging up ancient history. That's the trouble with old friends: they know too much.

Weren't always close. I'd play with Lynne, and Shirley would tag along. Then somehow it changed.

That time they came to my house, Lynne was so polite, like Mom was from outer space. Shirley said, "Your mother is beautiful."

I never invited Lynne around again. Didn't want my mother hurt by stares, smiles. She never was, or never showed it. Never showed it when my father got mad and shouted. Bastard. Didn't get me, though, not me.

The only time I saw her cry was when her mother died. I sat in her lap, tugged at her neck. "You still have me, Mummy. You'll always have me."

She tried to smile. "So much she did for me, my mother, so many things. Now I have no mother."

I buried my face in her sari, "Don't die, Mummy, don't. Mummy, I'm scared. Don't ever die."

She held me close. "Mala, listen, I will never die, because I am in you. You came from my body, so you are part of me. As long as you are alive, I will be alive in you." Her face lit. "And my mother will always be in me."

"And her mother was in her," I shouted. Like those Indian dolls she bought me, one inside another, bright yellows, reds, dark almond eyes, the same fixed, smiling mouth. Alike forever.

But I'm not like her, don't want to be. I'll never do the meek and suffering act for any fucking man, slave for the whims of some despot, duty, religion, whatever. *Yes, Mohan, no, Mohan, three bags full, Mohan.* I hate the way she ironed his shirts, cooked his meals, put up with his tantrums. Surprised she didn't wipe his bum. How could she want that for me? Ugly little man, strutting around, trying to look bigger. Hate the way she hovered.

Did she mind that I didn't cook Indian food? That I never spoke Hindi, never wore those saris she'd saved for me?

Yards of vibrant silk, petal softness. We'd dress up in them every now and again, Shirley and I. And occasionally her jewels.

Dress-up. That's all it was. Mostly in the late winter, when the drabness needed relief, when we thirsted for glowing colours. Before the ice broke in the strait, before the walks could start.

I pick up the shell.

Those early morning walks on the beach, that's when she was happiest, drinking in the morning air, the blue, her sari whipping bright in the wind.

We did that together, my mother and I. The day Barb and I fought about her birthday party, Mom said as we walked home from the beach, "It does not matter so much now, does it?" And it really didn't.

Sometimes I catch an unexpected glimpse of myself in the mirror. No sari, no *bindi*, no jewels, my hair's short, yet I see her. Sometimes I feel an expression on my face that I've seen on hers. At times my smell reminds me of her. When I hugged her, I'd get a gulp of ocean air, a trace of spices.

There's the faintest glow in the sky. Not light so much as the beginning of the absence of dark.

I climb out of bed, dress quietly. Shirley is sound asleep. A car roars by outside. Shirley must have opened the window.

The letter is lying exactly where Shirley put it down. No name written on it. I suppose she didn't dare. No name. For me.

I tiptoe to the table. Beside the daffodils is the box of *pedas*. Slowly, I open it. The *pedas* are dented with her fingerprint. I take out one, bite halfway into it, across the dent. The flavour of saffron bursts in my mouth. A heavy truck thunders by. I hear the tinkle of her bangles and the scrape of her spoon going around and around the pot, then quickly across the middle.

I tie my sneakers, pull on the sweater Shirley made me. There is no ocean here, but there is a park, green, still. No one goes there so early. There are waves and waves of daffodils and tulips. They'll open with the dawn, spill colour. I'll sit on a bench and gaze at them until they fill my eyes, fill them somehow. When there's enough light, I'll open her letter.

DOCTOR

THE TRAIN WAILS ONE LAST TIME and, slowly hissing, jerks forward. As we speed out of the station, I am riveted to the window. A woman in a tatty green sari flicks the nasal discharge of her half-naked child and stares after the train. It still fascinates me, the physical intimacy between a mother and child, which makes such a gesture commonplace here.

It's been twenty years. I always intended to return for a holiday sooner, but somehow, with my practice, I never got round to it. Perhaps I didn't miss India because I work in Wolverhampton and most of my patients are of Indian origin.

I take out my embroidery, a traditional English rose pattern, arrange the threads in separate colours beside me. Surprisingly, I have the compartment to myself. The other occupants discovered friends down the train. I relish the peace. None of the awkwardness of avoided glances, half-smiles, hesitant overtures before the inevitable deluge of intimacy with strangers. Indians ask the most unabashedly personal questions.

We break into the country, so familiar – flat parched land, stretching to the horizon, unrelieved except for some scrub and trees. The wires along a road running adjacent to the track dip and rise, dip and rise, and heat shimmers up. This, at least, has changed – the train is air-conditioned, the windows don't open, no grit in my hair, no pulsing heat, a subdued chugging rather than a noisy clatter.

❖

It is hot, dusty. The fan overhead does little more than stir the heat. Leaning out the window just brings a faceful of dirt and more heat.

Parvati's head is propped on her hand, her elbow sticks out the window. We are traveling north to the Himalayas. I have insisted she take a holiday. She is still pale and weak after her miscarriage, her second since Mala was born three years ago.

Parvati is more than a patient. There's a bond between us, though it can't exactly be called friendship. I suppose it's trust on her side, responsibility on mine, coupled with a curious protectiveness. I delivered Mala, swore she was premature, tended to her afterwards. Parvati knows I know, but we never discuss it.

I'm tired, too, body and mind. I wish we could snap our fingers and be there. I hate train journeys. My mind keeps drifting to Imogene. I have trouble calling her my mother. I don't know why I put her letter in my purse, I'm not going back to England. There's my work. Besides, Parvati needs this trip to the Himalayas and she also needs a doctor.

Dr. Kamla, who has an uncanny ability to hit the mark, said to me, out of the blue, "There are times when family is more important than work." She probably knew I'd received a couple of letters from England, and I suppose I haven't been quite myself lately. It's due more to the departure of my *chokri*, Asha, than anything else. Despite our ups and downs, we were used to each other. The new girl isn't as tidy, even if she is a better cook.

Parvati sighs and closes her eyes. She never discusses her family with me. She cannot possibly imagine how I understand. To her I am a doctor, she knows nothing of me, Bridget. She knows that I was born in India, lived here till I was six, but nothing of the flesh and blood, the things that count.

❖

I'm six years old and Mrs. Curtsley shows me the dorm I am to share with nine other girls.

66

"Sylvia is the dorm monitor. She will help you settle in."

Sylvia is tall, graceful. Her blonde hair is sleek and shiny, her hazel eyes cool, deep water. She smiles like a grown-up, with her lips closed.

"Welcome to Rushton Manor School," she says, leading me to the last bed in the room. It's by the door, opposite hers. There's a narrow wardrobe on one side and a small bedstand on the other.

"Can you unpack yourself or do you need help?"

I whisper, "I can manage, thank you."

"Good for you. Just ask if you're not sure about anything. It's lights out in three-quarters of an hour."

One by one, the girls introduce themselves. They're kind to me. They know I've come a long way, that it's my first time away from home.

In bed, in the dark, I hug my knees. I miss India, my father, my mother. All I've known is the spacious bungalow with the jungle lurking, the other officers and their wives, and the house full of servants. But most of all I miss Heera, who isn't really a servant. Heera is tall, well built, her arms firm, her sari crisp. She smells of Sunlight soap. She looked after me when I was born. She's been my ayah ever since. She helps me dress, combs my hair, sits with me during meals. I'm big now but Heera still holds me when I need her, never says I'm too old.

My mother is kind but remote. We walk together, and occasionally she reads to me, sometimes Shakespeare. I don't understand it, but I like the sound of her voice. I love watching her dress for parties. When she is ready, I am allowed to kiss her carefully. I wish I looked like her, but I'm like my father, sturdy, freckled, reddish-blonde. Everyone admires my mother, even the servants. She treats everyone with the same disinterested, gentle courtesy. Heera loves me best. Mother says she spoils me.

The night before I leave, I lie still under the mosquito net, pretending to sleep. My mother and father come in to check on me. They don't do this very often. My father says, "Poor little thing, she is so very little." My mother says, "She'll be fine, Ralph. After all, she's going home. Besides, she's getting too native."

I travel to England with a friend of mother's, who takes me to Aunt Aggie, who takes me to my new school.

At the station my father hugs me and says, "Chin up, Biddy."

My mother smiles her cool, beautiful smile, pecks me on the cheek and touches my hair lightly. Normally she is not a demonstrative person. "There's a good girl, no tears now."

The last night I cling to Heera and we both weep. Heera smooths the hair off my forehead, strokes my cheek. "Never mind, Missy Sahib. You will come back one day and I will still be here. You will come back."

The dorm is silent except for the shifting and squirming of nine other girls. At home there's always the susurration of insects, the distant sound of laughter from my parents' party, and Heera's soft, regular breathing. Tears squeeze out. I try to make no noise.

❖

I don't suspect right away that there is something seriously wrong at the Ungolis' house. I know Mrs. Ungoli works Parvati hard, but since Mala's birth, things have been better. I make unexpected visits, always inventing a valid medical reason. Currently, it's a benign growth on Mrs. Ungoli's left foot.

Mrs. Ungoli loves to feel important. She is short and stubby but mighty. She sits on a rope cot in the courtyard, her sari modestly tucked around her legs, the *pulloo* loosely draped around her back. She is an excellent overseer. She manages the house, her family, her servants, in fact, the entire village.

Mr. Ungoli is tall and skinny. He wears a *dhoti* and Nehru jacket and always carries an umbrella. It's his concession to vanity. That and his handlebar mustache. His hair is grey but his mustache remains black. He walks very straight and is reputed to be strict but honest with the peasants, a good *zamindar*. He detests corruption of any sort. "That is the trouble with this country, Dr. Bridget. These peasants will cheat and lie first without thinking. They can be using a little British honesty." He sniffs, his mustache twitching.

Mrs. Ungoli orders his favourite food, ensures he has his glass of cold *lussi* everyday at noon. Her voice, raised loud against anyone who displeases her, is soft with Mr. Ungoli. She knows the pecking order.

Parvati is barely higher than the servants. Her status has been raised by Mala's birth, even though Mala is a girl.

"We are not ignorant peasants only wanting boys," Mrs. Ungoli tells me.

Nevertheless, Parvati would have enjoyed a longer reprieve if she'd borne a son. It's been over three years since she's had a live baby. She's had one miscarriage, which has lowered her worth, but now she's pregnant again.

I'm concerned about her, beyond the fact that another pregnancy has followed so soon after her miscarriage. Her face appears troubled. I suspect that Mrs. Ungoli has stepped up the pressure on her. Parvati never says anything. Her husband, Mohan, certainly says nothing, and Mrs. Ungoli smiles smoothly and is never seriously unkind to Parvati in my presence.

Mr. Ungoli is always kind. "Come and sit with us, *beti,*" he says when Parvati serves the meals. But Mrs. Ungoli won't permit it. Mr. Ungoli is getting too free with modern ways.

I walk to the Ungoli house via circuitous routes in the hope of surprising them. Occasionally, in the early morning, I approach the house from the back. I see or hear nothing unusual. Sometimes, Mr. Ungoli is striding away from the back of the house and he waves to me.

Mrs. Ungoli is invariably pleased to see me. "Sit down, Dr. Bridget, sit. Parvati, bring some *chai* for the doctor." Her round face beams friendliness, her expression is guileless behind her cat's-eye glasses. The cat's miaow.

Parvati serves the tea, which Mrs. Ungoli calls for despite my protests, and I sit on the chair the servant brings. Parvati mostly huddles near the kitchen door. Occasionally, Mrs. Ungoli asks her to join us. She perches gingerly on the edge of the cot as if afraid to get comfortable. Once in a while, Mrs. Ungoli strokes her hair and praises some small accomplishment, a well-cooked meal, a piece of embroidery. I suspect it's for my benefit.

Mala, a round-eyed three-year-old, is always there. Sometimes when I examine Mrs. Ungoli's foot, Parvati combs Mala's hair. Mala howls if the tangles are bad. Then Parvati gathers her into her lap and rocks her, holding her close, smoothing her hand full against Mala's cheek as though she can't touch her enough.

The day I get the letters I'm later than usual setting out. Imogene's letter tells me she's sick, "a minor problem requiring minor surgery." She doesn't ask me to come back but she ends, "Do you remember the times you were little and I'd read Shakespeare to you? Your favourite was Portia's 'The quality of mercy'."

The other letter's from Aunt Aggie. She tells me about cancer and, in her tactful but less convoluted manner, suggests I come home. Of course, it's out of the question. My patients need me. Besides, my trip to the Himalayas is all booked. I can't possibly go back without seeing the Himalayas.

I take a shortcut to the Ungolis', and I arrive at the side of the courtyard. I see Parvati disappear into her quarters, her face red. I think I see tears.

Mrs. Ungoli is as welcoming as ever. I examine her foot and she says, "I know you are late so I suppose you don't have time for tea."

"Actually, I'd love a quick cup."

Mrs. Ungoli smiles and calls to Parvati.

Parvati is perfectly composed when she brings the tea, her hands steady.

"Why don't you join us, *soni beti*?" gushes Mrs. Ungoli.

Parvati sits at the edge of the cot, Mala in her lap. Mala tugs at Parvati's sari and the *pulloo* falls back from her face. Parvati's hair is damp from her morning bath. They're so faint on her cheek I almost don't notice, and even then I can't be sure they're really slap marks. Mrs. Ungoli is smiling, smooth as cream.

I've been at school for a month. I struggle with fierce torrents of homesickness, of missing Heera. I can't help crying at night. Other girls cry, too, but maybe because my bed's opposite hers, Sylvia hears only me.

At first it's cutting remarks: "Do you think, Bridget Parkinson, we could get through the night, just for once, without listening to your pig-like squeals?"

Then it's mocking my wardrobe during morning inspection, or making me brush my teeth three times, which makes me late for breakfast and in trouble with Mrs. Curtsley.

But it begins in earnest the night she asks why I'm sniveling, and I say I miss my ayah.

"Your ayah, your ayah. You great big baby, next thing you'll want your bottle. Fancy missing an Indian."

The following morning, during our free time in the Grace House common room, I read a book in the corner whilst the others play board games. No one asks me to join them.

Sylvia and some of the big girls are looking through an old book, *Roman Legends*. We all know that book, the s's look like f's.

"Listen to this," Jessie says aloud. " 'Romulus and Remus were fuckled by a wolf.' " They burst out laughing. I don't understand but I laugh too.

Sylvia looks at me and whispers something to another girl. "Pass it on," she says.

One by one, they whisper down to the next girl, convulsed with laughter. Finally, I'm the only one left.

"Say it aloud," says Sylvia.

Then laughing, giggling, they chorus, "Bridget Parkinson was suckled by a wog."

I take to visiting Parvati every day, sometimes twice a day. She's spotting, in danger of another miscarriage. She had a fragile stomach with all her pregnancies but she was never this withdrawn, fearful, nor her weight loss this rapid. I'm uncertain if she's afraid of losing her baby, or if she simply dreads her mother-in-law. I order complete bed rest. She needs it, but I also want her away from her mother-in-law.

Mrs. Ungoli supervises the servants attending to Parvati. Mr. Ungoli hovers, solicitous. Mohan is genuinely concerned. In his own way, I suppose he cares about his wife. Or hopes for a son.

Mrs. Ungoli tends to Mala more and more. And the child is attached to her. She sits in Mrs. Ungoli's lap, pinches her round face and Mrs. Ungoli laughs.

A week later, when Parvati is still bedbound, Mrs. Ungoli starts to complain about idleness.

"Is it really necessary, Dr. Bridget, for the girl to stay in bed all the time? Yes, yes, I know she is spotting, but other women have babies also. Peasant women don't lie around feeling sorry for themselves." The look she darts at Parvati is not loving.

I seldom get the chance to talk to Parvati alone. Mrs. Ungoli is always present. One morning when Mrs. Ungoli is in the *gussal-khana*, the bathroom, I ask Parvati pointblank if she is properly cared for when I'm not around.

She starts, then protests, "No, no, I am all right."

I lower my voice, "Something is obviously not all right. As your doctor I want to know what exactly is going on."

Her voice is a whisper. "It is nothing, Dr. Bridget." She hesitates. "It's just, the watching...." Her voice trails away as Mrs. Ungoli returns.

Sylvia returns from a shopping trip in the village, drops a box on her bed, and says to me, "I've got a surprise for you later."

The bell rings for supper, and we file down. It's Monday, shepherd's pie. While I struggle to eat, Sylvia looks at me as though there is something hugely amusing.

At bedtime she opens the box. "This is for you." She lifts out a golliwog. "See," she says nicely, "now you won't miss your ayah." She throws the golliwog at me.

The girls howl with laughter.

"Lights out," Mrs. Curtsley calls, coming down the hall. "Why on earth aren't you in bed, Bridget?"

Sylvia says, "It's all right, Mrs. Curtsley. She's just looking at a new toy I bought her."

Mrs. Curtsley smiles. "You spoil them far too much, my dear. You're a lucky little girl, Bridget. I hope you said thank you."

"Thank you, Sylvia."

"Don't mention it."

Mrs. Curtsley switches off the lights. I try so hard not to make any noise, but Sylvia hears, or if she hears nothing, guesses I'm crying.

"What's the matter?" she hisses, leaning over my bed.

I turn my face into the pillow.

Sylvia grabs my shoulder and lifts me. She places the golliwog next to me. "There," she whispers softly. "There's your ayah. Drink her milk." She pushes my head down, down.

❖

That evening, after I examine Parvati, I ask to speak to Mohan alone. We stand outside Parvati's room, in the courtyard. The dining-room door opposite us is open. Mr. Ungoli hitches his *dhoti,* sits down. Mrs. Ungoli bustles around serving dinner.

I tell Mohan his wife may have to be admitted to Najgulla Hospital. "She is losing weight far too rapidly. She is going to need an I.V. and we cannot administer that here."

He licks his lips. His voice is shaky. "But why she is not able to carry children? She was all right the first time."

"Yes, but Mala was premature. It's difficult to say what the problem is. Perhaps the climate disagrees with her."

"Are you suggesting we should move? Where? Najgulla?"

Najgulla is only thirty miles away.

"You might consider somewhere near the sea. Bombay, for instance. The medical facilities are excellent." The research company Mohan works for has its headquarters in Bombay.

Mohan runs his fingers through his hair and sighs. "That is a big change. If we are moving to Bombay, the climate may be better, but there will be no family to help look after Parvati."

In the dining room, Mr. Ungoli tears a huge piece of *chapati,* wraps it around a *bhaji* before putting it in his mouth. He eats as if he's starved.

"Of course, it's up to you, but I'm sure her condition will improve in Bombay. Perhaps sufficiently to bear sons."

When I get home, there's a letter from Miranda. She's really my cousin, but we grew up as sisters at Aunt Aggie's. She tells me about her honeymoon, goes on a bit too much about Simon, and writes, "Biddy, she's your mother. I know you're not close. I know she wasn't there for you when you were little, but she was an army officer's wife. She had to go where he went. For goodness sake, come home. She'll never ask, but she needs you. Anyway, you've been there four years. I can't imagine why you'd want to stay longer."

During the worst of it, I manage to send off one furtive letter to my mother. I'm not very old, I can't spell many words. Enough to beg her to let me come home.

The teachers are impatient with me. My appetite is poor; I cannot concentrate on my work; my eyelids are always raw. Sylvia says I look like a nasty, peeled shrimp. I wait for my mother's letter saying she is coming to take me away from here.

The dorm monitors often help us with the big words in our parents' letters.

Sylvia's face is only lightly amused as she grabs the letter I'm struggling with. "Dear Bridget, I'm sorry you are not enjoying school very much, but you must try to give it a good shot. We all miss you, but you have to be brave. Remember you are a soldier's daughter. We're going to the Himalayas for Christmas, to Simla. I'm sure you'll have a wonderful time with Aunt Aggie." There's more but I don't hear it. She ends her letter, "Heera sends her love and salaams to Missy Sahib."

Sylvia tosses the letter contemptuously on my bed. "Heera. That your ayah?"

I nod.

Sylvia lowers her voice. "That's what you're going to be when you

74

grow up, an ayah." She takes me to the mirror above the sink, points out my freckles with a sharp, jabbing forefinger. Her nail leaves curved indentations on my skin. "See, it's starting already. You were suckled by a wog so you've got black milk inside you. When you grow up, you'll be all black and you'll be an ayah."

That night I creep out of bed, run to the lavatory, and vomit. I've had a horrible dream. A dream that will recur throughout my childhood. I'm whipping someone while they scream. I don't want to see the face of the person I'm whipping, but occasionally I catch a glimpse. Sometimes, it's a thin face with pink-rimmed eyes, strangely familiar, sometimes unknown. But usually it's Heera.

❖

A servant from the Ungoli household hammers on my door at night. I rush to the Ungolis', the flashlight weaving.

There's nothing I can do to stop the miscarriage. Parvati is bleeding badly. I insist they fetch Dr. Kamla. Together we manage to staunch the flow. When we've cleaned up, and Parvati is sleeping, pale as a ghost, Mr and Mrs. Ungoli peep in at her.

Mrs. Ungoli shakes her head. "Poor girl. What is the matter with her that she keeps losing her babies?"

An Indian woman is not worth much if she cannot bear children.

The bed sheet is not quite over Parvati's shoulder. I lift it to smooth under her chin. For an instant the curve of her breast is visible. Mr. Ungoli is staring as I cover her up. His face is expressionless. He doesn't even blink. Only his mustache twitches.

Mrs. Ungoli's face hardens. "I don't know what is the matter with the girl, she cannot be having children." Her voice is sharp.

My hand shakes as I motion everyone out. I remember how I often see Mr. Ungoli around the back of the house where the *gussal-khana* is. The back wall is bent and warped. The morning I noticed slap marks on Parvati's cheek, her hair was damp from her bath. Mr. Ungoli always encourages her to sit with them. Mrs. Ungoli never permits it, keeps her busy with chores.

Mrs. Curtsley holds me after I tumble from my chair during break-fast. "Why on earth didn't you take her to Matron? The child's burn-ing up."

Sylvia's voice resonates integrity. "But she was absolutely fine this morning, Mrs. Curtsley, really she was."

It's bliss being in the sick room. Matron's clothes are stiff, starched. They rustle when she moves. In some ways she reminds me of Heera. But I don't think of Heera if I can help it.

After nearly two weeks there, Mrs. Curtsley says, "Well, Bridget, the doctor's given you a clean bill of health. Tomorrow, you may return to the dorm."

"Oh, Mrs. Curstley, no." I grab at her. "Don't make me go back, please. Sylvia – "

Mrs. Curtsley disengages her hand. "My dear child, do get a grip on yourself. I do not listen to tales."

When I fail to eat a good dinner that night, Matron sighs and shakes her head. "I hope you're not going to have a relapse."

After she's tucked me into bed, I stare at the glass-cased cabinet that houses Matron's medicines. There are glass jars with long names, bright red Mercurochrome, rusty brown tincture of iodine. One time I asked Matron for more of a tonic that tasted like cherries and she said, "Dear me, no, Bridget. Too much medicine will make you sick."

I creep out of bed. I stand on my tiptoes to turn the key on the cab-inet, but I can't quite reach.

Slowly, I drag a chair to the cabinet. The linoleum is shiny, the chair slides easily.

From Matron's room next door, the BBC announcer says some-thing about war in Europe.

My forehead is sticky by the time I reach the cabinet. I climb on the chair, turn the key, and swing open the door. One by one, I take down three of the smallest bottles. I carry them to the sink, pour a little from each into my glass. The room is so dark I can't make out the colour of the mixture. It smells sharp. I lift the glass, put my mouth to the rim. My eyes water, and involuntarily I lower the glass. Some of the mixture splashes on my hand. It burns. I drop the glass. My elbow knocks a bottle off the sink.

It's the loudest smash I've ever heard. I cry out as glass bites my legs, something burns my feet.

The light is on and Matron is there, without her cap, her hair loose around her face. I think it's pretty hair as she bends over me, screams, "Mrs. Curtsley, Mrs. Curtsley."

❖

Before I leave the Ungolis that night, I take Mohan aside and suggest that I take Parvati away for a holiday. "The air is too hot for her. A month in the Himalayas would be vastly beneficial."

He looks doubtful.

"If you want your wife to survive this miscarriage, you must let her get away from here."

"I can be taking her myself. There is no need for you...." He's remembered his job and that I'm a doctor.

"I'm going anyway. The arrangements are made, the accommodations booked. In the meantime, please consider our conversation yesterday. Bombay's climate will suit her better." I look him full in the face. "Your mother, I'm sure, will agree."

The next day I talk to Mrs. Ungoli as she sits on the cot at the head of the courtyard with Mala in her lap. I can't quite read her eyes behind those ridiculous cat's-eye glasses. Mr. Ungoli sits at the other end of the courtyard, within earshot, absorbed in his newspaper.

"For now," I tell Mrs. Ungoli, loudly, "no one is allowed to visit Parvati. She is seriously ill. Only you and the servant may tend to her. No one else. No visitors, not even family. She must have peace and quiet. Doctor's orders."

Mrs. Ungoli cuddles Mala in her lap. "Oh, yes, Dr. Bridget, don't you worry, I'll see no one disturbs her."

"I don't want her getting up even for a bath. A maidservant can sponge her daily."

"All right, Dr. Bridget, whatever you say. You are the doctor."
Mrs. Ungoli's eyes are bland. They never leave my face.

Mr. Ungoli hasn't turned a page in a long time.

Aunt Aggie comes to see me in the hospital. "You poor child, why didn't you write and tell me?" Her smile is sweet, warm. "That's not fair, is it? After all, we barely know each other." She hugs me. She's my mother's sister, but she isn't afraid to touch me.

Mrs. Curtsley brings a box of chocolates and says, without quite meeting my eyes, "Bridget, dear, I wish I'd been told."

I don't go back to Rushton Manor. I go to a day school, live with Aunt Aggie and Uncle Graham and Miranda and Peter in Staffordshire. There are no servants here, just Mrs. Kenny, who comes in twice a week to clean. We children actually eat with the grown-ups, help with chores. Uncle Graham and Aunt Aggie take us out every Sunday on family outings. The countryside is splendid.

My mother and father return to England just before the war starts, but my father is with the Intelligence, in London, so I stay with Aunt Aggie.

Years later my mother hears from a friend who stayed that Heera died in a cholera epidemic. For me, she died long ago.

Parvati recovers in the fresh mountain air. Here, she feels safe, she can rest, but her eyes are still sad. She misses Mala. I get to know her a little better. Not by anything she says – she is too loyal – but by watching her face. I'm certain she doesn't understand her father-in-law's interest, never connects him with the person lurking and peeping outside the *gussalkhana*.

It's beautiful here, peaceful. It's good to feel a nip of cool on my cheeks, snuggle under blankets at night. Even so I have strange dreams that haven't troubled me in years. I walk a lot everyday. Parvati says, "Dr. Bridget, why you are always rushing around? Rest a little." But I can't. I love to walk, walk fast.

One night I dream I'm a baby, crying, and Heera is there, holding me, shushing me. She looks curiously like Parvati. A voice hisses, *drink her milk.* As she lifts me to her breast, I wake abruptly.

When we return to Barundabad, it is to the news that Mohan has been transferred to Bombay. They move in two weeks. Mr. Ungoli is away on an urgent business trip concerning Mrs. Ungoli's parents. He'll return only a few days before Mohan, Parvati, and Mala leave.

During the month I've been away, there are two more letters, one from Imogene and one from Miranda. Imogene's is characteristic. "I'm recovering nicely, and really, I'm eating so much I shall get positively fat."

I can't picture Imogene fat. She is tall and willowy. I've never seen a single photo of her pregnant with me, so I can't imagine her cool belly swollen and distended with child. Immaculate gestation.

Miranda's letter is also characteristic. "Biddy, if you don't come home now, you'll regret it the rest of your life." She adds in a postscript, "If your father were alive, you'd come. If it were my mother or I, you know you'd be here."

The night before they leave for Bombay I drop in to see the Ungolis. Mrs. Ungoli, with Mala in her lap, is in the courtyard, facing the setting sun. She smiles when she sees me.

"*Arré,* Dr. Bridget, it is good of you to come." She shouts for a servant to bring tea. I resign myself to an hour.

"Parvati," calls Mrs. Ungoli. "The doctor is here."

Parvati breaks away from her packing and joins us.

Mrs. Ungoli rocks Mala, gently caresses the top of Parvati's head. "What do you think of these children, leaving me? I will miss them."

Parvati lowers her forehead to her mother-in-law's feet. "I will miss you too, Mother."

Mrs. Ungoli lifts her up and embraces her.

Parvati's eyes are guileless as she says with apparent sincerity, "You have been like a mother to me."

I swallow a mouthful of acrid tea. I've never become accustomed to the Indian habit of letting it boil.

I work furiously the next week. The clinic is busier than usual. I sleep fitfully, disturbed by dreams. It's the searing pre-monsoon heat. The air is heavy with suppressed lightning. I long for the release of rain. Sylvia, Imogene, Mrs. Ungoli, I don't want to know. It's easier just to hate them.

One night lightning crackles. At last, healing rain. My parents went to the Himalayas, to Simla, that fall I spent in Rushton Manor. Both my parents. At night, Mrs. Ungoli sleeps with Mr. Ungoli. He owns the land, he is the *zamindar.* At night, Imogene slept with my father, he was the officer. I wrote to both of them. He didn't come either.

The next day I tender my resignation to Dr. Kamla, make arrangements for my journey home.

My mother lingers for two years, during which we see more of each other than ever before. By the time she dies, I am well established in my practice in Wolverhampton.

❖

As the sun fades outside, I switch on the light. Just a few green leaves left to embroider. A cluster of roses, it's a pleasing, harmonious arrangement.

I still hear from Parvati every Christmas. She always addresses me as Dr. Bridget, says she'll never forget what I did for her in Barundabad.

I pierce the needle through to the other side. Rather messier this, threads tangled, knotted, streaks of colour overlapping, crisscrossing from one patch to another.

I pull down the blind. Reflections from the compartment are disconcerting. I hope the other occupants return soon. When there's no one to talk to, the clacking of the train and the continuous motion seep into every cell. It'll reverberate through me for days.

Seed Pearls

Rekha's coming, rekha's coming, all these shadows rustling, all this noise and confusion, just because Rekha's coming.

That elephant Neela with her tight, tight clothes. Swish, swish, swish. No shame, that girl. Fat girls with thighs crashing together shouldn't wear pants. Parvati, at least she listened. No straying eyes, no showing off. I'll leave some jewels to her. Fat one and Vimmie-slut, they won't get so much as one ring.

Cold. Why do they leave me sitting in the shade? My bones are chilled.

"Ehhh! Fat one, come when I call. Come."

Footsteps, swish, swish, puffing. Hot hands on my shoulders.

"Yes, Mummy, what d'you want?"

"What d'you want, what d'you want? Don't you use that tone with me. Hours you leave me in the shade, in the wind. You know I get cold."

"Sorry, Mummy, but I'm busy, too, getting ready for Rekha's visit."

She calls the servant and they pull my cot into the sun. They're so rough I almost topple backwards. But I dig my fingers into fat one's arm, I don't give her the satisfaction of falling.

"Now get me a drink of water, quick."

Swish, swish, swish.

"And don't mutter."

Why Chetan married that fat woman I can't imagine. Must be difficult, two mounds like *luddoos,* one on top of the other, rolling off. No wonder they have no children.

Cold glass to my lips.

"*Luddoo.*"

"What, Mummy?"

"You're making *luddoo,* aren't you? I can smell *besan.* It's Mohan's favourite. When are they coming? Parvati's better than Vimmie-slut, better than you. When are they coming?"

"Mohan and Parvati aren't coming, Mummy. They're in Canada. Rekha's coming today. She and Prakash just got back from their trip to Canada, remember? She's coming specially to visit you, to bring presents from Mohan and Parvati."

"Don't shout, I'm not deaf. I know Rekha is coming, I simply asked: when are Mohan and Parvati coming?"

"Oh, Mummy, you're confused. They're not coming at all."

"Stupid girl, you understand nothing. Go, leave me alone."

Swish, swish swish.

"And get out of those pants. Your buttocks look like two *luddoos.*"

I know Mohan and Parvati aren't coming today, I know that, I remember they live in Canada. That fat one, she doesn't have to humour me. Mohan is in Canada, he married Parvati, she's not as bad as those other two. Ramesh is in Bombay with that Vimmie-slut, and I'm stuck with Chetan and his fat wife. Three sons, three little pigs, pampered wives drooling for me to die so they can grab my jewels.

Cotton. That's all I wore. They took my silks away, gave them to his sister. One by one, my jewels. A bride in cotton. Govind, they made him do it. They didn't want him pleased with me, didn't want his eyes on me, no.

That Gita, on the day of her marriage, wearing my heavy gold set, inlaid with rubies. My mother's mother had that made when she was married and his sister got it. Always hated that Gita. Poison. Laughing and whispering. They think I don't hear, but my hearing is good, it's always been good. Even on my wedding day, *how dark she is.*

She does it on purpose, his mother, sends me out in the sun. Wants me dark so he won't look at me.

Kali kalooti,
Baingan looti.
Black, black, blackerine,
Stolen from an aubergine.

No sun for Gita, oh no, cream on her face, and I'm sent outside all the time. But I'll be a good wife, wait and see, I'll be indispensable. He will look to me for everything. And those whispers I'll hoard. Every one, like a dagger.

My mother, years and years hoarding, silk saris, jewels, every birthday a new set, at thirteen the pearl necklace, strands of seed pearls, delicate as whispered wishes, fourteen my emeralds, fifteen the gold chain to my waist. So much money they've put away for my dowry, every man will want me. Sixteen, married. My grandmother's heavy gold set, inlaid with rubies.

Everything they took. My mother-in-law, hands rifling through the piles of silk. *I'll take care of these.* Never see them again. Except on Gita. My dowry in money, they buy land with that and then they take my jewels. For Gita. But I say nothing. I take care of his needs, I cook his favourite food, and I bear him sons. No daughters, three sons, yes, three, they can't say I don't bear sons. Patience. I am his wife, he is the only boy. One day it will be *my* house. I wait.

Blazing hot. I'll burn in the sun, blister. That's what they want.

"Mummy, what're you doing?"

Fat arm. Not my mother-in-law, her arm's like a stick. Chetan's wife, yes, Neela.

"What am I doing? Can't you see, owl, I'm trying to move. Why d'you drag me out in the sun? You want me to get dark, dry out?"

"But, Mummy, you wanted to be in the sun, remember?"

"That was hours ago."

"No, Mummy, it was only half an hour. And the next time you want to move, just call. I don't need you falling, on top of everything."

"Don't you shout at me. If I had my legs strong, I'd get a stick, lay it on you. Get me in the shade, stupid one."

"Mummy, you'd better go to your room, have a sleep before Rekha comes."

Sleep. My back's throbbing. Used to throb like that, pulling water from the well, the same spot, below my waist, to the left side, pincers digging into me, sweat pouring down my face, between my breasts.

She helps me to my room. Hard hands, that fat one.

"Now don't get into my things while I sleep."

"Mummy, no one wants to get into your things."

Bangles tinkling.

"Where did you get those?"

"Now what, Mummy?"

"The bangles, sly one."

"For goodness sake, Mummy, Chetan bought them for me, remember? On our fifth anniversary."

"Let me see." Grey. It's all grey. I touch them. Hard gold, but they're thinner than mine. I feel my arms. Bare. "Where are my bangles? What did you do with them?" My chest is tight, hurting.

"Oh, really, Mummy. You took them off, you said they were too heavy. They're right here in your room, all your jewelry, in your top bureau drawer, just where you put it."

Fat hands, hot on my back. Won't get my bangles, I put them away, yes, I locked the box, tucked the key inside my sari.

The sheet is cool, soothing.

"There, Mummy. Have a nice, long rest, won't you? You'll be all fresh for Rekha."

"Rekha. I didn't let Gita give her my jewels."

"No, Mummy. Gita isn't even coming. It's just her daughter, Rekha. Can't you remember?"

I remember. I remember everything. Gita getting married in my jewels. *See, what a handsome pair, so lovely Gita is, pity about that Madhur, brother's wife.*

How could I look nice for him, my thirteenth-birthday pearls gone, my silks, all gone? Cotton fading in the sun, burning me. *Kali kalooti.* Never call Parvati that. She is fair. Yet I never took anything away from her, never. I was a mother to her. See how I dressed her, a bride, always in silk, jewels. Parvati, even in the sun she doesn't burn. It is my house. My belly stretched bearing his sons, my breasts shrivelled like old mangoes, feeding his sons, he won't look at me.

84

She won't get my jewels, Parvati, she has enough. Eyes following her, in the sun, in the kitchen, everywhere.

Didn't follow me. I put *kajal* around my eyes, oil my hair, it is beautiful, long. I pray – my body, make it light, pleasing, fill my breasts. In the temple I pray for him. But they take away the jewels, leave nothing to catch his eyes.

He sees me for the first time on our wedding night. Afraid, the bed with flowers. He takes off the jewels, parts my jasmine veil. Looks away. *You must be tired.* Yes, I'm tired. Afraid. The next day, and the next, they look at the sheets. Whispers like cobwebs. He should not look away. I dress in silk, must wait. All these jewels I have, these silks, I can be lovely. A fine match, see how tall he is, how fair. My fault. Short, dark. Whispers, sticky, covering me. They want my blood, I am glad to endure *that* pain, just don't shame me.

He comes to me, not often. In the sun it's too bright, he's blinded, at night too dark. But my eyes, clear then, watch his every glance, anticipate his every need.

They send him. At the well, raging sun, sweat soaking through my cotton sari. So distant the glimmer of water in the well. He looks away. "You know those pearls? Gita needs them. And the gold and ruby set."

Gita, lilting, her husband's eyes on her, on my pearls. Gita whispering, *not pleasing, such a shame, kali kalooti.* I will stop those whispers, make them stop, spiders, all over me, crawling, light little legs, on my face, body, hands, crush them.

"Mummy, are you all right?"

"Who, who, who is it?" My heart, bursting.

"Mummy, it's Neela." Fat hands. Plump on my back.

Careful, breathe in, out, in, nice and slow, it's easy. I'm fine when I don't think of it. There, in, out, in.

"It's all right, Mummy. You must have had a bad dream. No, no, sit still."

"Let me get up, idiot. I must change out of this cotton. Govind always liked silk."

"Mummy, Daddy passed away years ago."

Govind. Eyes closed. Why doesn't she understand I remember?

"Oh, Mummy, don't cry. I'll get a nice cup of tea. You're just excited about Rekha's visit."

Tea. They treat me like a fool. I want to beat the lot of them, move, stop this crying. It's that Rekha's visit, confusing, all this fuss. It's my house still, she won't get my things, no one will, not Parvati, not Neela, never that Vimmie-slut with her fast Bombay ways. *Oh, Daddy, you're so funny!* Sitting in his lap, hugging him, slut, painted face, low blouse, leaning over him, dragging his eyes down.

"Here's the tea, Mummy. Let me hold it."

Hands aren't as steady as they used to be. I get frightened sometimes, grey wall pressing, but I won't have the operation, I won't leave my house. Tea, warm.

"D'you need anything else, Mummy? I must go and make sure the servants are cooking dinner properly. Rekha's coming to visit, you know. Bringing presents from Mohan and Parvati."

"Yes, yes, I know. Just leave me in peace."

Swish, swish, swish.

"Take those pants off, your bum looks like two watermelons."

Rekha's coming. Gita's daughter.

Ha! My house. Gita's daughter had to get married in my house. Stupid Gita, never did prayers for her husband on *Karvachauth,* too busy rushing off to Bombay parties, dancing, drinking. No wonder he died.

I told Govind, *It's your duty to have the marriage here. Poor Rekha has no father, a girl should be married from her father's home, or her uncle's.* I've always done my duty, yes.

Rekha married here, the biggest, best wedding the village has ever seen. Thousands and thousands of rupees we spent. Feasting for days, still we threw out piles of food. Those Bombayites won't look down on us, say I neglected his widowed sister's only daughter. Poor Gita. No sons. She doesn't call me *kali kalooti* anymore, oh no, she is respectful. It is my house.

The night before the wedding I go to her room. I smile. *Remember those jewels I loaned you when you got married?* She isn't laughing now.

Cotton they dressed me in, thin, cheap cotton, took all my silks, all my jewels.

86

But I'm kind. Oh, yes. I lend Rekha jewels for the wedding. I even let her keep one necklace. Bloodstone. A gift from me. Gita doesn't have a lot to give her daughter. Should have gone to the temple on *Karvachauth*.

Yes, Gita, I get up in the dark, eat before sunrise. I fast all day. I eat nothing until I glimpse the moon. And I pray. My husband has a long, prosperous life. Again and again I pray. His mother won't live forever.

Poor Mummy, stroke, bed bound. I take care of her like a daughter. I dress her, comb her hair, such tangles, how her hair comes out in clumps. So sad she can't speak. Look how her eyes follow me everywhere. Even as I sort her saris, jewels.

I never took anything from her. *Mummy, you want me to have this, don't you?* See, she gave it to me. No one will take it away from me again. No one.

Pots and pans banging, such commotion. How can I sleep? Smells, *basmati* rice, *parathas, halva, gajar ka halva*. Someone's coming. Rekha. Married here. She wore my jewels. She won't get them, no. Top drawer, they're safe.

Sari drags my legs. Yes, the box is in the top drawer. Key, open box. My thirteenth-birthday seed pearls, my bangles, my heavy gold set with rubies, those diamond earrings he gave. Can't keep standing. Wait for heart to steady. Wet, she spilt tea on me. Rings don't fit. No matter, the first knuckle will do. There, all my jewels, on my arms, ears, throat, on my hair, hands. They'll remember whose house this is.

"Mummy! Look at you. What a sight!" Swish, swish, swish. Fat one.

"Get out! Who told you to come in here?"

"Oh, honestly, the smell. Can't you even remember to call someone to take you to the bathroom?"

They give me drinks, forget, all to humiliate me.

Strong hands, pulling, pinching, taking my jewels.

I hit her and hit her, scream.

Hands like vices. "That's enough, Mummy. You'll get hurt. You have to get changed."

87

She's stripping my gold bangles, my seed pearls, my rings, my sari, scolding, air cold on my skin, I can't breathe, she's taking everything.

"And stop that silly crying."

Car horn, voices.

"Rekha. Already. Oh, what am I going to do with you? Here, you'll have to wait."

Cotton sheet around me, running, swish, swish, swish.

I free my hands of the sheet. Hard, my jewels scattered on the bed. I snatch them together, press them to my belly. I'll put them on again, every one, I'll kill her if she stops me. Rings, gold chain, bangles. My seed pearls. I grab and grab, but they slip through my fingers.

Auspicious Day

Mutton curry for dinner. Quickly, quickly, I put the finishing touches to the red purse I'm embroidering. It's my favourite time of day, when the work is almost done and I plan our evening meal. A special feast, today. Mutton curry, two *bhajis, jallebie* and....

In the corner, a slow shifting. That Sundri. Why must she go sneaking, sneaking? Aren't I a good sister, patient, kind? Creeping off behind the curtain in her corner of the hut. She's changing her sari, putting on her lightest one, the grey. She'd wear white, that one, except I cut up her white saris – it's high time she stopped that mourning nonsense.

Grey sari. Sliding along the wall like a mouse.

I keep my eyes on my work. When she's almost at the door I clear my throat. "And where're you off to?"

Sundri jumps, says in a high voice, "I thought I'd go to the market, Asha. I ... I saw some nice squash. Might as well get it before it's all gone."

I smile nicely. "No need. I already bought some."

Sundri wrings her *pulloo,* shifts from one foot to the other. "All right then. I'm going for a walk."

"In this heat, fat woman, at your age?"

"I'll take a bus."

"Bus? Where?"

"Oh ... anywhere."

"Anywhere! D'you think I'm stupid? Look at my hair. Look, it didn't get grey in the sun."

Sundri stands there, blinking, blinking.

"Go on then. Get out of my sight."

Sundri wipes her eyes, hurries away, head low, shoulders hunched, the sun beating on the back of her neck.

"Cover your head, *chakram.* You'll get sunstroke." Then I yell, "I'll have a feast ready when you get back."

Sundri's face turns, shocked.

I laugh. Every year on this day I say that. Nineteen years and still she's shocked.

Oh, I've no patience with her. Running to the temple, crying over Tilak. Might as well pray for the soul of every dead cockroach. How many times do I have to tell her and tell her? This is an auspicious day. It's unlucky to mourn – she'll only bring ill fortune down on our heads.

So much to be thankful for: electricity in the hut, a fan for hot days, a radio, the extra room we've built. Everything's nice and clean and we've enough to eat.

Me, I wear my brightest sari, my red with the round mirrors embroidered in green. I put flowers in my hair. I cook a feast and I eat heartily. Isn't this the day that Rekha Sahib got married, a day of feasting for the entire village? Isn't this the day I moved back with Sundri, the day our fortune turned for the better?

Rekha Sahib's wedding, Rekha Sahib's wedding. That's all I've been hearing for weeks. She's getting married at her Uncle Ungoli Sahib's house in Barundabad. It's going to be the grandest event ever. They're going to feed as many poor as turn up. In the shop where I work, everyone is planning to go.

I'm finishing my sewing fast, fast, thinking about all that food, when Mahendar brings me a message from Sundri. She needs my help again. Tilak's really sick. Someone has to look after him and the children – she has to be at Ungoli Sahib's night and day for the wedding, and if she can't go, she'll lose her job and then how will the children eat?

That Sundri. How many times have I reminded her of what our

father used to say? *It isn't the cloth you're born with that matters so much as how you cut it.* Do I complain about sackcloth? No, I cut carefully, stitch with good stout thread, patch with velvet, silk, cotton, anything. Sundri, so clumsy, big holes, hardly a handful of threads – yet blinking and complaining if anyone tries to hand her a patch.

Hasn't Doctorsahib Kamla said again and again, no more babies? Eight in eleven years, eight. Lucky only four survive. They were even giving away transistor radios. A transistor radio! For a little tiny cut on his balls. But no. *It's his man's pride, Asha. He doesn't want his juices drying out.*

Dry. Make me spit. Always into *daroo,* passing out on the floor. But never too drunk to poke her. Then she blames *me,* picks a fight with *me.* I told her and told her, I only had my knife out to kill a cockroach near Tilak's dick. Fine sister. Practically kicks me out of her hut. Said we'd always be together when our parents died, but the only time she remembers me is when Tilak beats her up for her money. No concern how I might be getting along, alone in a big, evil city. *Think of the children, Asha, nothing to eat, Asha. Kuttai kai bucchai,* down my throat picking, picking my guts.

I take the bus to Barundabad and all the way I worry. How sick is Tilak this time? If things don't get better soon, Sundri and the children will suck me dry. I don't believe in praying all the time like that Sundri, but on the way to her hut I pray and pray and pray.

And there's Tilak, slumped in the corner of the hut, across the entire family's bedclothes. No sign of diarrhea, rotting lungs, not even a touch of leprosy. Big and strong he looks, a tiny, tiny tickle in his throat.

The state of the hut! Filthy floor, dirty pots, flies crawling over the baby, her bum, her face, everywhere. And the stink. Vomit, *daroo,* tobacco, sweat, piss.

Sundri. She's crouched in the corner, looking like a sack of bones a vulture would shit on. Sagging pot belly, hunched back, Meena at her withered breast.

Tilak moans for something to drink. Sundri turns to Ramu. He's only ten, skinny, big eyes, sores on his arms and legs, wearing short, ragged pants. He brings water from the well.

Tilak flings the tin cup across the hut. "What's this? Doctorsahib said I need medicine, not water. How can I get better?" He cuffs Ramu across the face.

Ramu howls. The baby lets go Sundri's nipple, then Priya and Dev start up. Sundri just sits there, unmoving, her stupid neck bowed. A fine, hearty welcome for her only sister.

I hitch up my sari, tuck the *pulloo* into my waist. "Look at this place," I shout. "It isn't fit for a cockroach. Ramu, take Priya and Dev outside. Wash them properly. Sundri, go sit in the shade, quick, out. I'll clean up, get a meal cooked."

Sundri sits still.

"What's the matter with you? Move, I said."

She looks at Tilak. "He likes to have me near," she whispers. "I know how to look after him."

I almost flatten her on the spot. But if anything happens to her, who'll take care of the children?

I say nicely, "Sundri, he's your husband, isn't he? Doesn't that make him my brother? How can I not take good care of my brother? Make your mind easy, go outside."

It'd be easier to burn the dump, but I start to clean. Chuddi and some of the other village women come by to talk, but I never stop. I fetch water from the well, make a fresh broom, sweep the floor, scrape the dirt off it, scrub the walls, scour the pots, gather the few miserable clothes scattered around. I have plenty of time to see how sick Tilak really is. Twisting and cursing in his corner. What good are prayers?

The children come back, noses running, whining like mosquitos. I look in the battered tins in which Sundri keeps her food. Not a speck of *atta*, a grain of rice.

Sundri blinks her starving cow's eyes at me. "Please, Asha, I'm begging. For the sake of the children."

Money, money, always wanting my money. Where's her concern now for Tilak's pride? Tilak is snoring.

And just then, a good omen. Music from Rekha Sahib's wedding, sweet, cool, a promise of plenty. My father used to say: *Always watch how others around you cut their cloths. Sometimes, if their cloth is ample, they toss out scraps. Make the most of them.*

"Take the children to the Ungoli house, Sundri. All that food's sitting there."

"But the feast doesn't start till later. And how can I work with children to look after?"

I cross my arms. "Always thinking about yourself, yourself. How d'you expect poor Tilak to get better with children crying and shouting? Go. I'll stay and take care of him. It's about time somebody did. Ramu, you wait, I have work for you."

Sundri looks at Tilak, blinks.

I smile. "Sundri, didn't I say I'll look after him like a sister? I'll lavish him with care. I promise. On our mother's memory."

Sundri drags herself out, carrying Meena, with Priya and Dev clinging.

"Ramu, go fill this bucket with water."

When he leaves, I cover my head with my sari, go to the corner of the hut. Tilak is still snoring. Vomit in the sun smells better.

I stir him with my foot.

"What? What is it?" He scratches his groin. His dick sticks out like a rotten cucumber. He rubs his face, smacks his lips. His breath stinks, his eyes are red, pus in the corners, his face bristly with a trail of drool trickling down one side.

I shake my head sorrowfully. "Oh, Tilak. Now, we've had our differences, but I won't insult you by giving Sundri money behind your back. You're the man of the house. Here. You need medicine."

I press the rupees in his hand.

Tilak quickly counts them, grins. His teeth are rotten. "I always knew you liked me, Asha." He farts.

Tears come to my eyes. "Aren't you my brother, Tilak?"

I take the dirty clothes to the river. The women, their washing done, are leaving.

"Asha," they shout, "come to the feast."

The smell of *halva* wafts tantalizingly towards me, but I say, "I can't. I have to take care of Tilak. He's very sick."

Halfway through washing the clothes, Ramu comes running down. He's crying and crying.

"*Masi*, he gave me money, but he won't let me get food. He wants me to get – "

93

"That's enough, Ramu. I can't stand disrespect. He's your father. Obey him."

He just stands there, tears spilling over.

"Go," I shout. "Stop looking at me like an owl. Do as he says."

When I get back to the hut, Ramu is sitting outside, his face sulky.

"All right, Ramu. Run to the wedding. Eat all you can. But bring food for us. Quickly. And as much as you can carry."

I spread the clothes to dry on the bush and go inside the hut. Tilak is tilting a bottle to his mouth. A plain bottle. It smells strong.

"Is that your medicine?"

"Yes, yes. My medicine." Tilak empties the bottle. There are five full bottles beside him. "Doctorsahib said the more the better."

"Poor Tilak. It must taste awful. But be brave. Drink it all. Nothing is more important than your health."

I sit outside the hut mending clothes. So what if my money is gone? I'm helping Tilak, aren't I? Won't that benefit Sundri and the children? Me? I wave to people going to the feast and sing loudly about sisterly love.

At sunset, Ramu comes back carrying a huge plaintain leaf from which food spills in a crooked trail behind him. Crows, cawing with joy, pounce on it.

"*Masi, Masi,*" he shrills. "So much food. It's a feast." His eyes gleam.

I open the plaintain leaf. *Pullao, parathas, bhajis,* all richly dripping *ghee,* enough for three people. There are even some sweets, *halva, jallebie,* sticky, mixed with the food. My mouth is watering, watering, but how can I eat with Tilak wasting away in the hut? I pop one small piece of *paratha* in my mouth.

"Take it all to your father, then get back to the wedding. Bring more food. Nice and rich, mind, as much as possible."

Pain in my belly. I take a *lota* of water and squat behind a bush. When I finish, I clean myself with my left hand.

In the hut, the heat is like a blanket of steam, the stench stronger than ever, mixed with the sharp smell of Tilak's medicine.

The oil is low in the lamp but I light it. Flies, buzzing and bumbling, swarm over the food. Tilak is drinking from a new bottle.

94

"*Arré,* Tilak. All this lovely food, and you're not eating."

I help him sit. His eyes are half-closed. "Come on, open your mouth. We don't want you dying of hunger." I shove in a handful of food with my left hand. Some of the rice spills down his face. I scrape it off his bristles into his mouth. Somehow, feeding him takes my hunger away. "Oh, don't spit it out. You must eat, get your strength back." Tilak keeps saying he's had enough, but I make sure he gets every last bit of that food down his gullet.

"That's good. Lie down and drink more medicine. I'll be right outside the door."

I wash my hands thoroughly, blow out the lamp. If it tilts and the hut catches fire, Tilak is so big, I won't be able to drag him out. But there isn't a lot of oil and anyway Sundri and the children will have nowhere to live. I'm careful.

Lights from Rekha Sahib's wedding, red, blue, green, gold, dance and twinkle with the music. Laughter drifts down with the fragrance of *basmati* rice. There'll be tables groaning with food. Sundri and the children will eat as never before. People passing by call me to go to the feast with them, but I sit still, head covered with my sari, hands together, and pray aloud for Tilak.

Tilak moans for Sundri.

I light the lamp, bend over him.

"Yes, brother, what is it?"

"Thirsty. Water."

Still three bottles of medicine unopened. "Oh, Tilak. Water doesn't do any good. Didn't Doctorsahib say the more medicine the better? How else will you get well?" I tilt the medicine into his mouth. I make sure he gets plenty. He sputters, coughs, swats at the flies.

"Look at these flies bothering you. And you're sweating like a pig. Next thing you'll get a chill, catch your death of cold."

I wrap all the heaviest covers around him. "There, nice and snug. Now drink more medicine."

It's completely dark when Ramu comes back, this time with two plaintain leaves. Priya and Dev are with him. What can Sundri be thinking?

95

"Ramu, take your bedrolls. Go back. Tell your mother to put the children to sleep in the Ungoli house somewhere. Your poor father is just starting to rest. I can't allow them to disturb him."

The children leave, delighted to be returning to the feast.

Oh, the food, it smells so good, so good. But Tilak comes first. Didn't I promise Sundri? I wrap a clean cloth around one plantain leaf to keep out ants and flies and take the other inside the hut. I light the lamp.

"Sit up, Tilak. Time to eat."

He moans.

"Poor Tilak. So weak you can't even sit? Come, you have to fill your stomach. Never mind, I'll feed you lying down."

I thrust a handful of food in his mouth. He turns his head away. "Tilak, it's your sister, Asha. Open your mouth. It's for your own good." He keeps turning his head from side to side but quickly, quickly, I get every bit of that food down him.

"Now for your medicine." I lift his head. "Drink it all. For Sundri and the children's sake. You can do it, that's it." He's still sweating, sweating. I wrap the covers tightly around him, lay him flat on his back.

At last, my turn to eat. I wash my hands properly three times, sit outside, open my plaintain leaf. Such choice, rich food. And so much of it. Tilak is making strange noises, gurgling. At least he isn't coughing. A tender piece of mutton. Soft, juicy, rich with *ghee*. Wheezing noises from Tilak. He must have something in his chest. Caulifower *bhaji*. *Shrikant*, the flavour of saffron. Less wheezing now. I save a piece of *jallebie* for last. Sweet, dripping with syrup. No more wheezing. Praise God, Tilak is cured. I lick my fingers clean, wipe my tongue caressingly along the leaf. Delicious.

I put away the finished purse and wash my hands. I start the mutton curry, the eggplant *bhaji*, then cook the squash with onions, tomatoes, and spices.

So much good fortune in the past nineteen years. Our work sells fast. We've managed to save money. Ramu, a taxi driver in Bombay; Priya, married to a shopkeeper; Dev, working in the new tire factory; and Meena, selling our work in the market in Najgulla. Sundri, she'd love to marry Meena off. *What's a woman without a husband?*

Never learns, that Sundri. How she smiled when Bahadur Lal started to pay *her* attention. Fast, fast, I put a stop to it. Told her straight out I wouldn't allow any disrespect to poor Tilak's memory.

That whole dutiful widow bit she went through at first – wearing white, breaking her bangles, smearing her *bindi,* wailing and pulling her hair. But she started to eat again, oh yes, when I gave her two hard slaps, told her I wasn't going to get stuck with her children.

Great one for crying, Sundri. *Remember what our father used to say: How you cut your cloth affects you not only in this life but the next one as well.*

It's the one thing my father said that makes no sense. People with velvet and satin may have time to sit around worrying, worrying about the next life, but I'm busy enough trying to get by in this life. Anyway, if there's any truth to it, I should come back a *rani.* Yes, rich in silk, with fountains, music, lights, and platters of food.

Now for the *jallebie.* My favourite. I squeeze the batter into hot oil. I boil spices with sugar and water for the syrup.

Oh the smells! I can hardly wait to roll a *jallebie* round and round my tongue, feel that syrup squirting down my throat. It isn't every day I get such pleasure. Sundri, she can do her mumbo-jumbo prayers to remember Tilak. Me, I prefer to eat.

Moon Snails

Just when they call for passengers to proceed through security, Nina starts to wail and cling. I hold her tight, kiss her cheek, still sticky with blackberry jam, and try to hand her to Jake.

"Mummy, I want you," shrieks Nina.

Jake pries Nina's fingers off my neck, kisses me hurriedly. I can barely hear him. "Take care, Mala. Call as soon as you can. Don't worry, we'll be fine." He jiggles Nina in his arms in a futile attempt to quieten her. As I go through the security gate, I can still hear her howling.

It's an Air India flight, en route from Bombay to Toronto, the only one I could get on quickly. I'm seated next to a young bride. She must be from a village, decked out in a swishing, orange-and-gold taffeta sari with a harsh, brassy glitter. She's wearing bangles, necklaces, rings. Her hands are stained with henna, and there are wilting marigolds in her hair. I meet her eyes fleetingly and look away. Despite myself, I feel pity and embarrassment for her. She is so bright-eyed, eager, grotesque in her finery. Rushing to the promise of indoor plumbing, wall-to-wall, videos.

I scrape a drop of something that looks suspiciously like egg yolk off the leg of my jeans. The girl stares and smiles. I flash a brief smile and close my eyes. I'm incapable of making small talk. I'm annoyed at feeling slightly guilty.

99

❖

Those calls always come in the middle of the night. I notice the time is 3:03 as I drag myself out of bed and run for the phone in the kitchen. I pull Nina's door shut on the way.

"Sunil?" I'm so fogged with sleep I can't understand why my brother in Brandon, Manitoba, is calling. Even when he says he's calling from P.E.I., my first thought is he's drunk.

Jake switches on the kitchen light. I blink at the sudden brightness. Jake's hair is tousled. He is tying on his bathrobe, his face and body alert. I'm starting to register what Sunil is saying.

"When?"

"This afternoon."

"Is he...?"

"No, he's in intensive care."

There is a long pause. I wait for Sunil to say something. The only thing I want to say is *So?* or *Thanks for calling.*

Sunil sighs. "Mala. Can you come?"

I hadn't expected this. "Come? There? What's the point?"

"Christ, Mala, don't start, not now. Please."

I say carefully, "Who wants me to come?"

"We all do. Mom does. He's unconscious, for heaven's sake."

"Look, Sunil, I'm sorry for you and Arun and Mom, but it's a bit much. I'm in England. It costs money."

I realize my mistake when he says, "We'll wire you the money."

"Yeah, well, it's not just that. I can't drop my life. I have Nina, my work."

Silence at the other end.

"Where's Mom?"

"In the hospital. Arun's with her."

"Well, give her my love."

"God, you're a bitch."

"Thanks a lot. In case you don't remember, I don't owe him – "

"Yeah, yeah. Have a nice life." He hangs up.

My hand is shaking as I replace the receiver.

"Mala?" Jake touches my face gently. I push his hand away and sit down at the table.

Jake fills the kettle and turns on the burner, the hiss of gas. I stare at the floor, the orange linoleum we all hate, the circular pattern in what Jake calls vomit-yellow. The circles overlap. We've lived here for a year and I never noticed that.

Jake hands me mint tea, rubs his forefinger along the inside of my arm.

I grip his hand. "Hey, how 'bout that? All along I've been saying he's the kind that'll never have a heart attack, just give 'em."

"Not funny, love."

"Oh, when you go on about your parents I'm supposed to laugh, but now it's not funny." I pull my hand away.

"Look, you can't pretend it means nothing."

"Forget it. Let's get back to bed."

I let Jake answer the phone the next time. He comes into the bedroom, switches on the light. "It's for you."

My mother's voice is tired.

"All right, Mom, because *you* need me."

I hang up, drag the hair off my face. I start to laugh. I can't help it. "D'you know how clichéed this is? What do they expect, a deathbed reconciliation? It's like a B movie."

"Mala, he's dying...."

"So, big deal. It's not like I'm suddenly going to notice his absence. I'm not a hypocrite."

He shakes his head. "Sometimes you terrify me."

I swing around, my voice sharp. "You know what terrifies me? I knew something like this was inevitable. I've always prayed that Mom wouldn't be the one, because then I'd never see her, she'd never see Nina...."

Jake holds me.

❖

When Nina was born, Mom called from Arun's place in Halifax. They didn't visit Halifax often, but each time they did, she took the opportunity to call. Of course, she'd heard of Nina's birth from Sunil and Arun.

Arun lures him out with, "Come on, Dad, let's go get a real cappuccino."

I can imagine Mom, waiting for the footsteps to fade before dialing with eager, fumbling fingers.

She is in tears on the phone. "Mala, I'm so happy. Your first baby, my first grandchild."

"Mom, I wish you could be here. England isn't so far. Why don't you come?"

With Nina's birth I feel the need for my mother, feel it as never before. I don't mind so much that she's never met Jake, but I want her to see Nina.

"It's all right, Mom. Don't worry. I'll send Sunil and Arun pictures of the baby, lots and lots, and you'll get to see them. Oh, and Jake sends his love."

After I hang up I feel weepy. Jake explains my anger at my father as postpartum blues.

Arun visits when Nina is two months old. He brings a letter from Mom. She sends a silver bangle for Nina. "This was yours when you were little," she writes. "It was in the safety deposit box."

When Jake and I got married, Mom sent a pair of old-fashioned half-moon pearl earrings. Also from the safety deposit box. It had to be something rarely worn.

Mom's letter conveys no message from anyone. She leaves it to Arun to do that.

"Listen, don't freak out," says Arun gruffly. "After Nina was born, Mom told Dad."

Jake looks up from the fabric collages he's making for Nina, beautiful colours, textures – silk, velvet, taffeta, corduroy.

"So he knows she's been keeping in touch?" I'm nursing Nina so I don't raise my voice.

"She just said she'd heard of Nina's birth from us."

I try not to tense.

Arun flashes a small grin. "It was quite the scene."

"Did she tell him to fuck off?"

Arun grins again. "She begged him to reconsider."

"Ha!" Sharp as a whip. Nina jumps, starts to cry. "Shh! Sorry baby." I rock her gently. She grumbles and fusses before latching on again.

102

When Nina is finished, Jake says, "I'll burp her and get her changed. Come on, sweetie." He holds her soft gangly head against his neck. I love his face as he looks at her.

I pull up the flap of my bra, clip it on.

"And what did the little bastard say?"

"Oh, come on, he's not that bad."

I laugh. It is unpleasant, even to my ears.

"Okay, he is a bit of a jerk."

"Tell it like it is, Arun. He's a fuckin' asshole."

"I don't want to get into that." He looks at me defiantly. "I know, he's a sexist pig, but – "

"Where is this getting us?"

"He does care for Mom. When she told him about Nina, and he saw how upset she was, he said there could be a reconciliation if – if you apologize." He rushes the last words.

"Me? Me, apologize to him?" Waves of anger ripple my face. "When hell freezes over." I point my finger at Arun. "You tell the little bastard he'll have to come crawling over broken glass before I'll forgive him. And tell Mom she's got a home with us any time she wants to leave him."

The next time Mom manages to call, Nina is four months old. We don't mention him.

"Excuse me, ma'am." It's a flight attendant with a fixed, painted smile. "Would you like a drink before lunch?"

I order a gin and tonic.

When the bride rustles towards me and smiles shyly, I hesitate, then smile back. I need the distraction.

"Is it your first time coming to Canada?" She speaks with a strong Indian accent.

"No, I grew up there."

"Oh, you are lucky. It is my first time. I am only just getting married. My husband is living in Toronto." She pauses. "You are also from India, no?"

I just told her I grew up in Canada. Can't she see the difference in our clothes, the way we talk?

When we lived in Canada and people asked what my nationality was I'd say, "Canadian. What's yours?" *Where are you from?* In England, it's easy, *From Canada.*

I nod curtly, then overcompensate with a smile I regret as she bombards me with questions through lunch. She's convinced she'll live happily ever after in Canada, wallowing in wealth.

What do I tell her? She probably doesn't even know her husband. How can she understand what it'll be like having children there? Watching them fit in, spat upon, rejected, rejecting their parents to fit in. Set apart, little brown tiles in a mosaic, twirling with the other tiles, exotic costumes, dances, food. *Gee I love your culture. What country are you from?*

As soon as lunch is done, I bury myself in a magazine.

When the plane nears Toronto, I gaze out the window. The lake, the spruces sharp against the sky, it's so familiar, as though etched on my retinas. But despite this tug, elation, I'd turn the plane back if I could. Mistake, letting them talk me into this journey.

When we land, I stride quickly off the plane, avoiding the bride's eye. I can't be responsible for her. It's not like I'm with her. In the terminal building, she stands still, gaping. I turn back. She'll face enough snubs. I help her through Customs, then rush to the Air Canada counter.

It's familiar, Toronto, the voices soft after years of clipped British accents. I find my way easily, my body unexpectedly relaxed, my tongue sliding comfortably into the drawl. I wait to catch my flight on standby, get on.

Toronto to Montreal, then Halifax, then P.E.I. There is no eager bride to occupy me now. Just a heavy-jowled businessman who takes up more than his share of the armrest.

I sit rigid. You can't hate someone for years, construct it carefully, brick by brick, then suddenly knock it down, sob and wail. Like those ghastly sing-song obituaries people insert in papers on death anniversaries. Paragons of virtue, every one. You live a mean, spiteful life, but when you die – hey! you're perfect.

I won't be the first to hold out my hand. It's important, even now. Maybe there were too many years when my life was cramped and warped by his frenzy to lock me in his prison for good Indian girls. Too many years hiding the anger, the fear, that paralyzing fear of parental power. I'm of age now.

As I come through the arrival gate in Charlottetown, Sunil is waiting. He looks as if he hasn't slept for a week. He hugs me hard, suggests we go straight to the hospital so I can talk Mom into coming home for the night. *He's* still in intensive care. They don't know if he'll pull through.

It's strange to be here again. The airport's different. There's a new hospital, not the two previous, one for Catholics, one for Protestants. We drive in silence. My stomach is knotted. It's hard when you're with someone who's grieving, in crisis, not to pick it up. It's almost tangible, thick, soupy.

In the intensive care unit, I insist on waiting outside the door while Sunil gets Mom.

She rushes out. "Mala."

This is why I've come. We cling, sway, cling, weep. My mother's hair is lined with grey, her skin dryer, less firm and elastic than before. I remind myself why I haven't seen her in thirteen years.

Mom looks at me, smooths her hand on my face. I'd forgotten that gesture.

"Come," she says.

I can't speak. I'm horribly afraid I'll cry again, but I will not go in there.

❖

In the night, I wake suddenly. It takes a few seconds to remember where I am. I switch on the bedside light, peer out the window. I can just make out the strait beyond the spruces.

I don't know how long I've been sitting at the window when the door opens. In the dim light, Mom looks like a young girl with her loose dressing gown, her hair plaited down her back.

"Mala?"

"I couldn't sleep."

She touches my cheek. I hate the tightening in my throat, so I put my arms around her, lean against her waist.

She holds me close, then pulls away. "There's something I have to tell you." She takes my hand. We sit on the bed. I will not be quenched in her urgency, grief.

Her voice is low. "What I am going to tell you I have told no one else, except my mother." She looks away briefly. "When I got married, I was already pregnant with you. He is not your real father – never mind who is – but Mohan is not your biological father. He does not know. No one knows. Marrying him saved my life in India. And yours. Always I have been grateful. Shh! Let me finish. He has regretted what happened with you, many times he has. You know what he is. Right or wrong, Mala, he cannot say sorry to you." She stills my hand. "I am not asking you to. No I am not. But he saved our lives. Show some pity now."

It's the fatigue. My head spins. Her words drop like stones, I see them flung, the delay before they fall.

I shake my head.

Her lips tighten. "You want revenge? Go and tell him you are not his daughter. You hate him. Go and tell him."

For a long moment I stare at her.

"It is true, Mala. I would not tell such a lie."

Two figures on the bed, such a story being told. Again she lifts her hand to my face. It's real, her flesh warm pressing my cheek.

"Mom?"

"I would not tell such a lie." There is pain, confusion in her eyes.

It can't be true. My mother, the perfect wife. Not my father. Cuckold. All these years.

A crack of laughter escapes me.

❖

The day after the funeral I scramble down the path to the beach. I've missed this.

It'll take time to sort and sift the changes. There's the inevitable miasma of sentimentality after a funeral.

So many people, didn't know he'd forged that many links. In the end, thrown into the fire, not by me, a Hindu funeral, sort of. He wanted his ashes sprinkled here and in India, in the Ganges. But the ceremony was a mixture, a Hindu priest and, surprisingly, one hymn. It was his favourite in the British-run school he attended as a boy. I can't quite picture him singing it.

He who would valiant be
'Gainst all disaster
Let him in constancy
Follow the Master
There's no discouragement
Shall make him once relent
His first avowed intent
To be a pilgrim.

One minute here, the next minute gone. I told Jake that the shock of seeing me killed him. Mala the shrimp killer. I laugh aloud. It's sick, but Jake understands. Miss him, miss Nina, her prattle.

I pick up a moon snail shell, walk on, searching for more.

What if I hadn't come, hadn't gone in? My father, not my father. Somehow, it makes no difference.

In the hospital room, the ogre, a shriveled bag of bones. All these years larger than life, and all this time he was shrinking. So easy to snap, fling into the fire. Defenseless without the glasses, bald, tufts of hair about the ears, wispy, like a baby's. Those old, incestuous fears. Bastard, would have sacrificed me on the altar of his Indianness. Poor bastard. Never opened his eyes. What could I say?

Why couldn't it be simple? The one decisive confrontation of my fantasies, victory, release. It'll take years, damn him. It would have anyway.

But I can shed the burden of my mother as the perfect wife, impossible, fanatical virtue. She's more real now. We've always loved each other, maybe, with time, we'll understand. Someday I'll ask her.

I have a handful of moon snail shells. I flop down on the sand, arrange them in a straight line, small to largest.

So much I didn't see. Nina has power over me. Why did I never make the connection? Sunil's had girlfriends, and Arun, mostly white. Thought it was because they were boys that he didn't hit the roof. Only partly. Afraid of losing all his children.

I gather the moon snail shells, arrange them in a spiral, the smallest in the centre.

So little I know about him. A collage of drab, rough scraps. A workaholic, rasping, rigid. It'll be different with Nina and Jake. Those collages he makes for her, she loves them. Her favourite is one of the sunset, crimson-and-blue moiré silk.

I, too, have my crimson-and-blue moiré silk – in Bombay, once in a very long while we get out together. Mom stays in the flat with Sunil, who is just a baby. We stroll down to Chowpatti and he buys us *gol guppa, bhelpuri.*

"How hot d'you want it?" he asks.

"Oh, hot, Daddy, really hot!" I eat until I'm dizzy.

Then he laughs. "Next time we'll get it milder, no?" We get a coconut hacked open for us and drink the sweet, quenching milk.

I have to search for such scraps.

And in Canada still a workaholic. One trip that first year, to an ice cream parlour.

My father says, "We'll come here regularly, like we used to go to Chowpatti."

It takes a long time to get our ice cream. I feel my father getting restless, angry, and something else I can't name.

When we finally get our cones, I say, "Daddy, that man forgot to say, *Thank you come again,* like he did to the others."

My father says nothing. In the pit of my stomach I realize he feels shame. I can't finish my mocha ice cream. It runs down my arm, streaking it brown, and my father is angry at me. We never go out for ice cream again.

These days I cry easily. And laugh.

I rearrange the shells in a semi-circle, like a necklace, largest in the centre, tapering outwards to smallest.

Wonder how the bride is getting along.

My parents, were they eager like her, convinced they'd find something better? He used to talk about leaving behind the corruption, the caste riots. What did they expect of the promised land? A thousand and one flavours of ice cream, trickling away, sour, sticky. Sticking to old familiar ways, poor bastard, trying to straddle two continents. No man's land – here, not quite home, there, more and more unfamiliar. Continental drift. You have to choose. Or split. Yet they stayed.

I remember so little of India, fragments. Sunil and Arun remember nothing. Less torn, easier fitting in.

When I get back to London, Jake and I will look for jobs back in Canada. This is home. The most home I know.

Strange convolutions, so many wasted loops of time, years of tortuous anger, coming to this uneasy understanding. Still so many to spiral through. Even after he's gone, he devours my time, energy. Jake says I must be patient.

Never knew him very well, not the smooth stretches of memory I have with Mom. Don't know if I ever liked him. Right this minute I don't hate him. He dies, I have my mother back. I'm grateful. It's enough.

I scoop up the moon snail shells. There's a trace of dampness in some. I examine them carefully. They still have snails inside. The tide's low. It's a long walk across the sandbars. I throw the shells with the snails into the sea, put the empty ones in my pocket, and hurry back.

PARVATI'S DANCE

How do i tell her story? Do I tell it as she told me, pitiful, skeletal, the edifice of their love gutted, steel girders gaping? Or the way it seemed to her then, rose-and-ivory marble?

If I weren't her daughter, if *he* weren't my father, would she have told me more? She doesn't understand – I've spent years hating the man I knew as my father. It's effortless to hate an unknown.

But even if she isn't constrained by that, she is by habit. We have no precedent for discussing the intimate details of life. It also prevents me from asking certain questions.

She starts with a sigh. *So young I was, so silly.* Silly, how? *Romantic,* she says.

She is eighteen, she's been closely guarded in an Indian household, a world where love isn't mentioned, just duty. Premarital sex is a fate worse than death, dating unknown. She'll have an arranged marriage. Her mother never mentions sex to her, not the biological aspects, let alone desire, tongue, clitoris. She is, according to a documentary I once saw on India, a perfect Indian girl, *a vegetarian virgin.*

So where did she get those romantic ideas? The outside world creeps in only through books and films. She reads romances, *Mills and Boons,* from England. Her mother permits this as a vehicle for improving her English. And she sees Hindi films, as many as she can, particularly when she's in college. In her home town, there's only one cinema, and her mother never lets her go unless she's accompanied by a friend or a maidservant. Most of her friends are married off, and her maidservant, Isabel, a Goanese Christian, like most servants, isn't any company at all. In Najgulla, where she goes to college, there are three cinemas.

When I was young, my father – the man I called my father – and other members of the Indian community would occasionally arrange showings of Hindi films. Mostly, my mother made some excuse not to accompany us. She didn't care for the films, she'd say. They were too escapist; she preferred to stay rooted in reality.

My brothers and I sat at the back of the hall with the other kids, making gagging, choking noises at the grotesqueries on screen. All I remember of the movies is they were impossibly romantic: boy meets girl, parents forbid, villain tries to ravish, boy rescues, parents consent, happy ending. And lots of singing and dancing.

I look through the photograph album, find one black-and-white snapshot of my mother when she went to college. She's wearing her best silk sari, a green one, she tells me. She's squinting at the photographer, head tilted to one side, hands fiddling with the braid that hangs over her shoulder, down to her waist. Entwined in her hair is a garland of small white flowers. Jasmine. There is a half-smile on her face.

I get a magnifying glass, look at the picture more carefully. Her eyes, I want to read the expression. Shy, hopeful. Is there a hint of something more, a wistful eagerness?

Does she daydream about love, sex? Does she feel hot urges between her legs? Does she think masturbation is a sin and confine her fantasies to what she's seen in Hindi films, searing glances, chaste embraces, no kisses?

Today, here, she'd have a quick fuck and that'd be the end of it. Not then, in India. They check the sheets for signs of blood. *A vegetarian virgin.*

So silly I was. My mother, alone for the first time, studying Domestic Science in a ladies' college in Najgulla, guarded by nuns who teach at the college, who do know the world, curious paradox. Curfews, no one allowed out alone unless the nuns know exactly where they're headed, and why; no men allowed in.

Yet she managed to meet him.

I have to tear it out of her, pieces here, little bits there. She doesn't look at me as she speaks. Her head is low. She answers my questions hesitantly, and as briefly as possible. On her face is shame. And anger. At him or at herself, for believing so easily?

My mother was arranging a marriage for me. She pauses. I don't ask, but I surmise it was to the man she married, Mohan. *I wanted more. I wanted Romance.* She says it with a capital R.

Surely she didn't expect something like in the Indian films. She couldn't have believed those improbable plots. I look again at the photograph. Eyes shy, hopeful. Wistful, eager. Caged, frantic?

I met a man.

Met? How? They have all those Rules. Once she told me they weren't even allowed to use nail polish. Sometimes they use *maindi*, henna, to stain their hands and feet, but nail polish is modern, daring.

It was an accident.

After many questions, I piece together some kind of scene.

Parvati lingers as she comes out of the local cinema house. The afternoon sun is blinding after the gloom indoors. She straightens her sari, smooths her hair, humming the plaintive love song from the film.

She's reluctant to return to the hustle and filth of the city. She has time before her dance lesson. Maybe she'll go to the library for some more *Mills and Boon* romances.

She swings her handbag onto her shoulder. Someone lurches against her, the bag goes flying, the contents scatter.

She turns around hotly. In a big city like Najgulla, there are men who deliberately bang into women.

"I'm so sorry. It was very clumsy of me," a light, male voice says in English.

Parvati looks up. He is tall, fair, handsome. Like a film star.

❖

I thought it was karma.

Her closest friend in college, Sushma, laughs at Hindi films so Parvati slips out alone. This is contrary to the nuns' rules, but Parvati manages it by combining her outing with her Indian dance lesson, occasionally skipping the lesson. She's taken these lessons for years at her mother's insistence. Classical Indian dance, *Bharata Natyam.*

I saw performances of *Bharata Natyam* when I was very young. I have vague memories of gorgeous jewelry and costumes, thumping structured movements, expressive hands, eyes.

She doesn't like the formality of the dance; she prefers the dancing in Hindi films, it's more spontaneous.

In the Hindi films I've seen, the dancing consists of running around trees, exaggerated facial expressions, poor miming. My brothers and I would re-enact the romantic scenes, hysterical, helpless with laughter

I thought it was karma. My mother was arranging a marriage for me.

❖

She leaves the cinema, hurriedly crossing the road, dodging honking cars and rickshaws. Posters of film stars plaster the walls on both sides of her. She glances nervously behind. He's staring after her. What cheek, suggesting he should drive her home. She's not that kind of girl.

Still, there is a certain exhilaration. There's no question he's handsome. Unlike that Mohan Ungoli her mother keeps pushing – Mohan may be rich and *foreign-returned,* but he's short, puny, dark. And he lives in a backwards village where there isn't even one cinema.

Girls in films manage to meet handsome, wonderful men, combine duty and love.

❖

Does she think about the stranger all week? Does she hope he'll be there again? Does she dress in her best green silk sari, outline her eyes with *kajal,* dot her *bindi* carefully, maybe even buy a jasmine garland for her hair?

He is there the next week, waiting, apologetic. He frightened her off the first time by suggesting he drive her home. This time he's deferential, polite, no sudden moves.

He's there every week. He is slow and careful in establishing the bond. After the film, perhaps he suggests an ice cream or cold drink, maybe in a Western-style restaurant where they serve tea in cups and saucers, not glasses.

She won't talk much about this time, when she dreams, allows the fantasies to bloom. Perhaps her skin glows and people stare as she walks with an extra lightness. Perhaps, in her cell in the college, her hands explore secret crevices. Is she frightened or exultant?

They meet twice a week. She's abandoned her classical dance lessons.

❖

That cynical friend, Sushma, doesn't she suspect, question her? Maybe she comes in one day when Parvati is dressing.

"Wow, look at you! Who are you all dressed up for?"

"Don't be silly. I always like to dress nicely." Parvati is tying on a pink-and-cream chiffon sari. It's his favourite, accentuates her curves.

"Yeah, you've been dressing up a lot lately. And going out alone a lot." Sushma giggles and winks.

"Don't be so horrible." Parvati flushes. "I'm not one of those trashy Anglo girls, getting up to God knows what."

Sushma's face sobers. "I know you're not. That's why I'm worried. I hope you're not doing anything silly."

"Oh, go away. It's nothing like that."

When Sushma leaves, Parvati slumps on her bed. Why does

Sushma have to make it sound degrading, frightening? He's kind, understanding, and always respectful. He's never even tried to touch her. His clothes, his handsome, fair face, his English, all declare him to be a successful businessman. He lives in Bombay, where the film stars live, but he's in Najgulla on an extended business trip with Mr. Farthington, the English textile tycoon. He's staying at the Farthington mansion, even uses the Farthington car.

Everyone in Najgulla knows of the Farthingtons. Their factory provides work for hundreds. Parvati has never seen Mr. Farthington, but she saw Mrs. Farthington distantly once. She has that contained air of importance, of knowing her worth. She travels in the back seat of a sleek imported car.

Parvati feels she, too, can be like Mrs. Farthington, important, contained, worthy.

❖

Two months of bliss, Mohan forgotten. Two months of marble castles, ivory, rose.

But in the end I was tricked.

In Hindi films, it happens occasionally to a secondary character, but never the heroine.

She doesn't tell me why she agrees to marry him secretly. Does her mother tell her how keen Mohan is? Perhaps her father writes, ordering her to marry. They can't afford an enormous dowry. Marriage to Mohan is better than their wildest hopes. He is from the wealthiest family in Barundabad; she's lucky she's attracted him. Their horoscopes are beautifully compatible.

The hero, the girl, the unsympathetic parents, and Mohan the villain. There are always trials before *happily ever after.*

Don't her parents know she's at that dangerous age? Don't they see it in her eyes? Look, it's right there in the photograph. Why don't the nuns suspect? Why aren't they more diligent?

There's no way I can reach through those spirals of time, save her that grief. There's no one to stop her.

A private Hindu ceremony, for God's sake. No one else is there.

116

Of course, no parents. Hers are out of the question. His are dead, he says. Why isn't the skeptical Sushma there? She never thinks of that. Her only concern is that she doesn't have enough money to buy a red silk sari. She probably wears her best green silk, and a jasmine garland in her hair. He'll buy her jewels and silks later, he says. It isn't proper now, not respectful to her parents.

And the marriage is consummated. Is it hasty, fumbled, in a park, or the car perhaps? Does he take her to a seedy hotel, rent by the hour? Maybe she lies again to the nuns, says she has to be away for the weekend, go home to meet a man her parents want her to marry. She could forge a letter from them. The old lessons of duty are sufficiently ground in for her to obey her husband unquestioningly.

Is he gentle? Does he take time? She's never seen a man naked, though she's probably seen some creep exposing himself. She has no idea what exactly to expect. Some elaborate dance, perhaps, on cool marble floors. I hope there is tenderness, ecstasy. I can't ask.

But in the end I was tricked.

How? Is there no such thing as a private Hindu marriage? Is he already married? Does he simply disappear?

Her voice is careful, her eyes guarded. I don't want her to relive the pain, but I need to know.

He was not who he said he was. He was not a Hindu.

There is no marriage certificate, just the traditional religious ceremony, hands bound, around the fire seven times.

What is he? He can't be Muslim. He'd be circumcised, even she'd notice that.

He was not a Hindu. Or of the right class.

Class. To her it is infinitely more insurmountable than religion. Rich and poor are galaxies apart. Imagine my mother, a gently-brought-up young woman, living in a hut with dirt floors, working in a field. She's always had servants.

But he's decently dressed, speaks English, he must have some education. So who is he? A clerk working for Mr. Farthington, impossibly poor?

A Christian. A Goanese Christian.

She's been married five days. She's back in college. He says she must finish the year, get her certificate. There are only a few weeks to go. Then they'll tell her parents. Meanwhile, they'll see each other as they did before, twice a week.

On the evening of the fifth day, restless and hot, Parvati goes for a long walk. She meanders through the cool, rich streets of Najgulla where huge, arching trees afford some shade. So many magnificant houses, some with turrets. She must see the Farthington mansion, be near him.

She stops outside the house and peers in past the iron bars. The next time he comes here, she might be with him, staying at that house. It has imposing marble pillars and a garden that's lush despite the water shortage. Her parents' house in Chotakhan is a mere fraction the size and they have three servants.

❖

I'd like to leave her there, soft-eyed, dreaming, let everything turn out all right. Her parents relent when they see how well placed he is, how devoted. And they live happily ever after, barring the usual ups and downs of life.

But a movement near the house disturbs the stillness. The Farthington car driving up to the front door.

Parvati crosses the road. It won't do to hang around outside the gate as the car emerges.

At the end of the driveway, the chauffeur opens the gate. He's smartly uniformed with a peaked cap. Parvati looks covertly at Mr. and Mrs. Farthington in the back seat, then her eyes glide by, stop, fix.

The chauffeur.

Close-up of her face. Shock, disbelief, horror.

He gets back in the car and drives through, then climbs out again to shut the gate. He does not look at her.

Mrs. Farthington's voice drifts through the open window. "Who is that lady? Why is she staring at you, William?"

"I don't know, madam, I've never seen her before."

❖

In a Hindi film I saw, a woman, upon her husband's death in a house fire, falls to the ground, smashes her glass bangles. Rose, purple, yellow, green, rainbow shards fly. She smears the *bindi* on her forehead, a crimson gash.

There's a wonderful shot of her prostrate on the pavement while behind her flames crackle and twist like a widow's fire. Sirens blare, fire engines streak by, crowds gape as the burning mansion collapses.

Of course, her husband somehow manages to escape and, searching through the charred remains of the house, discovers a hidden treasure. The last scene shows them clasped in each others' arms while behind them springs a bigger, better mansion.

❖

My mother, stumbling home alone, doesn't even know I'm inside her. I'm too small to hold her.

OTHER BOOKS FROM SECOND STORY PRESS:

Aunt Fred is a Witch *Gilmore*

The Amazing Adventure of LittleFish *Hébert*

As For the Sky, Falling:
A Critical Look at Psychiatry and Suffering *Supeene*

Beyond Hope *Zaremba*

Canadian Feminism and the Law:
The Women's Legal Education and Action Fund and the
Pursuit of Equality *Razack*

The Extraordinary Ordinary Everything Room *Tregebov*

Ezzie's Emerald *McDonnell*

Frictions: Stories by Women *Tregebov*

Franny and the Music Girl *Hearn*

In the Name of the Fathers:
The Story Behind Child Custody *Crean*

Infertility: Old Myths, New Meanings *Rehner*

A Monster in My Cereal *Hébert*

Menopause: A Well Woman Book *Montreal Health Press*

Pornography and the Sex Crisis *Cole*

A Reason to Kill *Zaremba*

Sudden Miracles: Eight Women Poets *Tregebov*

The Summer Kid *Levy*

Uneasy Lies *Zaremba*

WhenIwasalittlegirl *Gilmore*

Work for a Million *Zaremba*

The Y Chromosome *Gom*